R *Battle in the Night*

Jackson. Race expected it. His mind hadn't been idle while he'd been locked up. He knew Jackson had to kill him and why he'd waited until now.

Race shifted direction and rose to a crouch, gripping the meathook by its lighter end, ready to throw it at the next breath of movement from Jackson.

Then it came—Jackson's whisper, taunting, trying to trip Race into exposing his position while he shifted locations.

Jackson could afford to wait, but Race couldn't. He heaved the iron at the sound of Jackson's voice, following close on it with a leap, arms widespread. The hook missed Jackson, but Race didn't. He slammed Jackson back into the mud and heard the man's gun slosh away.

HORSETHIEF
TRAIL

I

Race Evans hunkered by the deadfall, despair tugging at his shoulders. He cast a glance toward the rapidly approaching snow clouds, then stood. Once more he worked his runover bootheel into the decaying wood of the fallen tree. He bent and sifted through the broken chunks and came up with maybe a half dozen fat grubs.

Some hell of a supper.

As he waited for the queasy protest of his stomach to settle down, unwanted memories flashed through his mind, memories of two hungry kids scrounging through garbage heaps on the fringes of trail towns.

He forced the picture from his mind and concentrated on the lay of the country round about. He had drifted through this corner of Buckskin Mountain about eleven years ago on his return from a drive up to Cheyenne. The Indians had called the place "Kaibab," their word for mountain lying on its side.

Race pulled his hat down hard against the wind and awkwardly mounted the mare. He stood a moment in the stirrups. From what he could make out, he guessed he had crossed the Utah line into Northern Arizona, but it wasn't something to lay a month's wages on.

With the suddenness of a broncs first jump out of the chute, the sky broke apart dumping its load of snow with such wild force the mare rared back in fright. Race was blinded himself by the smothering buttermilk mass and clung to the mare while she fought it out. The animal was too jaded, however, to really kick any lids off and he soon had her back under control. Dismounting, Race spoke soothingly to her.

"Easy, girl. Settle down. Easy, now."

He struggled the quivering animal past the skeleton stand of aspens into the deeper protection of the pines. Shivering with cold he pressed close against the buckskin, his thoughts grim.

Hardship wasn't something new to him and he realized just how desperate his situation had become. After Swan had let him go, he had started working south, hoping to land a berth with another outfit before the weather broke.

Too late now, he thought bitterly. Up until that damn snipe-gutted mustang broke him up bad a few months ago, he'd been doing better than the average puncher, with ambitions toward a spread of his own some day. As tophand and bronc peeler he'd managed to squirrel enough away to buy this buckskin broodmare.

Well, he wasn't the only one hurting these days. The whole damn cattle business was hurting. Heavy winter-kill last year. Drought this summer and fall. Once those stringy underfed beeves started flooding the markets, prices fell out.

Why, hell! No wonder a dozen out-of-work punchers had been waiting in his tracks ready to take up the slack.

But now, like that one time before, after years of scrimping and back-breaking labor, he had to start all over again. The only difference, this time he was ten years older.

The snowsquall died as abruptly as it had burst into life. But a new storm was developing to the northwest. With bleak humor Race eyed the churning mass and murmured, "Well, why the hell not?"

He tugged the reins and his horse followed headhung and spraddle-legged. Race shook his head. She didn't have much left in her either.

Loosening the front cinch, he stripped out the saddle blanket or what barely passed for one. The frazzled rag aggravated the saddlesores on the mare's back more than cushioned them—galls he himself had caused, riding to favor his bum leg.

Hell of a thing for a bronc snapper.

Race tore off a piece of the blanket to tie his hat down

against the wind and shrugged the remnant around his shoulders. The mare twinged against the pressure as he tightened the cinch.

For a moment the harsh planes of the cowboy's face softened and he roughed her mane in a gesture of sympathy. After that he walked the animal until his bad leg plain gave out and he had to ride. Almost apologetically he hauled into leather, swearing lightly under his breath. He set her into motion, their backs to the wind.

The storm dogged their heels the next hour. It caught them just as they reached a timbered gateway. A board hung from the log crossbeam, the brand HHH burned deep into it. Sleeving the snow from his face, Race saw another smaller sign nailed to one of the uprights.

The *Rafter Triple-H Connected* was a brand Race hadn't run across before, but that made no difference. Chances were they'd give him a place to bed down out of the storm and maybe some grub to boot.

Anticipation carried from rider to horse and the mare stepped out, new life to her dragging hooves.

In another twenty minutes Race came to a hogback. From its crest he caught a glimmer of light below. Because of a twenty-foot drop at the edge of the rise, he had to circle half-around the swale to reach the ranchhouse below.

But when he reached the yard, the house stood stark and lonely against the harsh gray overcast. A penned hound's lonesome howl announced his arrival, the only sign of life.

A sudden unease gripped him. Shrugging it off, he clambered up the half dozen ice-coated steps to the sideporch, and knocked on the door. After a reasonable wait, he knocked again.

Still not drawing a response, he walked around the porch's gallery to try the other doors. A frown creased his forehead. He could have sworn he'd seen a light down here from up on the ridge.

Having no better luck, he returned to the front. As he passed the front window, he caught a slight movement at it, or thought he did. He stopped and, shading his eyes with one hand, pressed his face against the pane, trying to peer inside. But he couldn't see beyond the lace curtains to the darkened interior.

Race leaned tiredly against the doorframe. He didn't even see any outbuildings, something unusual in an outfit this big. Best bet, he decided, would be to take the mare around to the lee of the building, hitch her there and come on back to the porch to wait. It was late afternoon and if no one showed by dark, he'd just crack out a window, go in, and to hell with it.

Reluctant to leave the modest shelter of the porch, Race lingered just a while longer, studying the building. He'd been used to jerrybuilt bunkhouses and lineshacks. But even his untrained eye could tell this place had been built more for utility than good looks.

Race shook his head, a faint smile creasing his lips. If nothing else, the place looked dry.

As he started down the steps, the veil of snow split long enough to reveal the dim outline of an outbuilding about a hundred yards out from the house. Sighing his relief, he took up the mare's reins and led her across the snow-covered yard.

The building turned out to be a medium-sized barn of the same log construction as the house's middle. A solid oak bar braced the double doors shut.

Fumbling with cold-numbed hands, Race finally worked the heavy beam up out of its traces. At that precise moment, a raspy voice from behind ordered:

"Freeze! Don't move and don't turn around!"

II

No doubt about it. Sage Hensen had caught herself a bull by the tail, and by the looks of him, a pretty rangey one. At first she felt pretty proud, the way she timed herself to the exact moment the stranger's hands were fully occupied before ordering, in as deep a voice as she could work up, *Freeze! Don't move and don't turn around*.

But now that she had him under her sights, what was she supposed to do with him? The scattergun shook in her hands.

She chanced a quick look in the direction of the house, but couldn't see it for the snow mist, let alone Libby or Jésus.

Libby, her older cousin, had seen him first, while Sage was engaged at the old pump organ. Then Libby's warning came:

"Sage . . . a rider back on the hill. Not one of ours."

Discordant overtones wheezed from the old organ as its bellowes emptied. In a flash she appeared at Libby's side, joined her in looking out the window. Rubbing steam from the glass, she asked, "Where?"

"He's looping around. You can't see him now."

"Jésus . . ." Sage called to the old Mexican casero, " . . . snuff out the lamps!"

Without wasting words, both women armed themselves, Libby with a .45 Peacemaker and Sage with the oversized shotgun. Even the old man pulled out a razor-honed *cuchillo*.

By the time Race had mounted the porch, the trio were ready and waiting. He didn't realize how close he had come to losing his head—when he peered into the window, Sage had been right behind the curtain and nearly jerked trigger.

As soon as he had quit the porch, they broke into quiet speculation.

What do you think? He looked drunk to me. See the way he walked? Think he's one of Farley's cutthroats? He's heading for the barn. If he's one of Farley's men, he could cut down on our crew without warning when they pull in tonight.

Sage grabbed up her cape and flung it around her shoulders. Hefting the clumsy scattergun, she raced out of the house, ignoring Libby's call. The stranger's irregular weavings across the yard were easy to follow. Then, while he fought the bar latch she slipped up behind. She had acted without thinking, now she was stuck.

"Ease off, son." Race's voice cut into her harried thoughts.

"Just stay right where you are." She still affected the gruff voice, but couldn't keep the tremor out of it.

Smiling to himself, Race thought, *some fool kid trying to act out the man.* In the same tone of voice he'd use to soothe any hammerheaded bronc, he said, "Just take it easy. I stopped up to the house but couldn't raise an answer. Just looking for a place to throw down out of the weather. This here's the Triple H?"

"3-H. How did you know?"

"Saw your brand over the gate back up the road a way."

Sage calculated swiftly. That meant the north road. Josh had been heading up that way earlier. Would he or the crew see this man's tracks. The storm probably had obliterated them.

"If you came over that road, you know this property is posted. I nailed up the no trespassing sign on that gatepost myself."

"What si—" Race started to ask, then remembered the little sign he couldn't read. Be damned if he'd alibi to some snotnosed little kid. Besides he was cold, his extended arms started to tremble under the weight of the oak beam and he was getting damn mad.

As Race shifted to ease some of the weight off his bad leg, the saddle blanket slipped off one shoulder. Automatically he grabbed for it.

At one with his move, the shotgun exploded at his feet.

"Hey!" He jumped, letting crossbar and blanket both flop into the snow.

"Why you damnfool! You could kill a man that way!"

"You've got the idea, cowboy. That was only a scare shot—next one won't be. Flip your gun out into the snow where I can see it."

"I'm not packing any damn hardware!"

Instead of arguing, Sage cocked the second hammer and nudged him in the back with the gun barrel.

Race began to swear, melting the air around him. With broadening drawl he used every cussword ever invented and a few too new to even be catalogued yet.

When he ran out, he snapped, "If you don't believe me, all you have to do is look for yourself . . . or go to hell . . . . I don't much give a goddamn which!"

Ears and face singed from the blistering, Sage edged forward. She braced the shotgun on one hip and reached out with her free hand. To get close enough to search him, she had to draw nearly against him, so that the double barrels of her gun were alongside of Race, covering the barn doors instead of him.

If Race hadn't been so damned mad, he'd have laughed aloud. The kid was as stupid as he was feisty.

Race dropped his arm and clamped it over the shotgun. At the same time he heaved himself backwards. The gun's second load triggered harmlessly into the barn door. The force of the blast gave added impetus to his hurtling body and the pair went hard to the ground with Race on top.

Ripping the gun free, he used it to jack himself to his feet, then spun to face the kid.

"Sweet Jesus . . . ."

Anxiously Race stepped back to her. "Here, let me help you." As he reached out to take her arms, his hand accidentally brushed her breast.

Pulling back against his hold, she snapped, "Keep your filthy hands off me!"

Startled into sudden obedience, Race let go. Sage plunged backwards landing heavily on her seat in the snow.

13

Her olive eyes crackled fury as she glared at Race. He just stared at her. You could count on one hand the number of decent women he'd ever been around and have fingers left over. But even he knew there were ways you didn't treat a girl of her caliber. Hell, plenty of men had been offered short ropes and long drops for less than he'd just done.

But once he saw she was all right, he was more amused than worried. Clamping his lips hard against a building grin, he again offered his hand. She brushed it aside and, with what dignity she could muster, lifted herself from the snow.

Race stepped back and watched as she brushed the snow from her clothes. She was sure enough a spirited little filly and nicely put together—as the saying went, built like a brick outhouse. Approval registered in his eyes.

Sage, however, was less impressed with him. Tilting her head, she returned his scrutiny of her look for defiant look. Just some raggedy-pants drifter. He even had rags wrapped around his boots—*California Moccasins*—but they looked as much to hold his boots together as to keep his feet from freezing. His canvas brush jacket was better suited to the mesa country farther south. He wore no chaps and his Levi's were threadbare to the point of immodesty.

She had some trouble making out his face. What the shapeless woolsey had didn't hide, several week's growth of whiskers did. Blisters lined the perimeter of his lips.

Sage wrinkled her nose. She'd heard about the kinds of things cowboys picked up around those houses of pleasure and wondered. Outside of the fact that the drifter was tall, towering well above her own five-feet-five-inches, Sage saw little of prepossession about the man and certainly nothing to recommend him.

During her appraisal of him, Race's temper shifted from amusement to a cross between embarrassment and anger.

"Ma'am," he said flatly, "I know I look all horns with the hair growed out, but I don't really eat little girls like you for breakfast."

"Really! You could have fooled me."

"Well, lady, anytime a woman takes chips in a man's

14

game, she'd better be ready to play by his rules." He'd been set to apologize for the language he'd used, for man-handling her, for *every* damn thing. But hell! That starchy attitude of hers riled him. How the hell was he supposed to know it was a woman bracing him and not some trigger-happy kid!

The two stared crossly at each other oblivious to the snow wildly whipping about them. Race shook his head. He sure picked a hell of a way to introduce himself to this outfit.

"Look. I didn't mean to scare you and I sure as . . . I sure never meant to rough you. It's work I'm hunting up, not trouble. I'd be obliged if you might could let me hang around long enough to meet the boss and hit him up for a job."

On a hunch, Sage suggested, "Why don't you try Kell Farley?"

The name caught Race by surprise. Recognition flickered briefly in his eyes before he veiled them. Kell Farley wasn't a name unknown to Race Evans. But that was another place and another time. Probably even a dif-ferent Kell Farley. He sure as God hoped so. He took too long to answer, strengthening Sage's suspicions.

"I guessed as much," she said. "You're one of Farley's greasy sack rustlers. You can march right back to him and tell him whatever his plan was, it didn't work."

"Lady, if the boss of this outfit turns me down, I'll sure enough look up this Farley. But I'm here now and a stranger to this neck of the woods, and—"

"—and you're a liar," she stated bluntly.

Race brushed the snow from his face with a ragged sleeve, too tired to argue. "You think whatever you want, ma'am. I'm still asking you to let me hole up in your barn till I talk to the boss."

Sage gestured toward the shotgun poised in Race's hand and asked in a maliciously sweet voice, "Are you giving me any choice?"

He handed her the shotgun and pointed out in a tone of voice equal to hers, "You've already throwed off both loads, *ma'am.*"

15

Sage bit her lip. "Look, even if what you claim is true—which I don't for a minute believe—this outfit is saddled with too many troubles of its own to take on a grub-line drifter like you."

Dirty, tired, half-froze and three-quarters starved, Race laid a long thoughtful glance on her before finally answering.

"All right, then, ma'am. I'll drift. Sorry to of troubled you."

During their little wrangle, the mare had crow-hopped back across the yard. Race's sparse movements as he picked up the blanket then trudged leaden-legged to his horse testified to the deep weariness in him.

As he caught up the buckskin's reins, he saw another woman up on the porch, a long-barrelled Peacemaker in her hand. She was looking beyond him, obviously for Sage. Seeing that Sage was safe, she lowered the gun to her side.

The cowboy shrugged wearily and hauled into leather. Both he and the mare were used up, but there was nothing for them here.

At the mare's first few faltering steps, Race knew he could not take her any farther. He eased back out of the saddle and for just a moment leaned his forehead down on it. Straightening, he began stripping the old rimfire hull off her back.

Sage, who'd been watching Race from a safe distance, moved toward him. That cowboy could have been faking, but his horse certainly wasn't. To set a man afoot in this kind of weather was tantamount to a death sentence. She couldn't do that—not even to one of Farley's men.

She called to Race just as he flung the saddle up over one shoulder. "Wait a minute, cowboy!"

Stiff-backed, Race turned to face her, waited patiently for her to speak.

"You can wait for Josh in the barn. Josh Hensen—my brother—he runs this outfit. But understand, just because I'm letting you wait for him is no guarantee that he'll even let you stay the night, let alone give you a job."

It seemed to take a while for what Sage said to register

with the cowboy. Then he relaxed. "Yes, ma'am, that'll be fine."

His obvious eagerness as he trailed behind her made Sage feel a little guilty. As he walked, he appeared to favor one leg. Could be he really was saddle weary. Maybe he hadn't lied about everything, she conceded to herself.

In contrast to the clamor of the storm, the barn was like stepping into a black vacuum. Once their eyes adjusted to the darkness, Sage pointed out an empty stall.

Race slung his saddle on top and led the buckskin in.

"I'll get some grain if you'll fork down the hay." She indicated the low loft just above and behind the line of stalls.

When she returned, Sage had a scrap of burlap with her and began rubbing the mare down.

Underneath the bucskin was a sound animal—good loin depth, straight strongly muscled legs, well-formed head. But too little flesh covered the broad angles at the hip points and across the barrel.

Sage discovered the saddle galls with her bare hand. She hurriedly scraped the drainage from her hand with the rag, thinking of the drifter's blistered mouth. A simple saddle pad or blanket could have prevented that. Then she remembered the blanket the drifter had draped around his shoulders.

Angrily she lifted her head toward Race still up in the loft.

"A man who doesn't take any better care of an animal than this doesn't deserve one."

A little self-consciously Race drew the blanket tighter over his thin jacket. Any explanation would sound like so much alibi-ing. So, to Sage's surprise, he agreed with her.

"Yes, ma'am. She's a fine hoss. Deserves a hell of a lot better than what I've been able to give her."

His answer had been softly drawled out, but carried enough of an edge to send chills through Sage and remind her just exactly where she was and with whom—in a darkened barn with a stranger who might be every bit as disreputable as he looked.

Anxious to get out of there, Sage called up to him, "You

can rest in the loft if you've a mind to, but be sure you don't light any matches or smoke up there."

Race nodded, then watched appreciatively as Sage swept out of the barn with the clean-limbed elegance of a thoroughbred.

The girl closed the barn doors behind her. And when Race heard her straining the heavy crossbar into place, locking him in, his lips parted in a bitter grin.

III

"Dammit, Jackson! Crap or get off the pot. You said first snow we run off them beeves of Hensen's."

Maize Jackson shot a piercing look at Kell Farley. The man's raunchy words were at sharp variance with his slight, almost effeminate appearance.

Small body, big mouth. Too bad he had to let Farley in on this deal. But he did need help to pull it off and Farley had the crew.

Patiently, Jackson explained, "This's just a little squall, Kell. Don't amount to beans. What we are looking for is something to cover the sign of 1500 head, not to leave a trail a blindfolded buffalo could follow."

"What the hell difference? Let Hensen follow. Counting you and the Injun, we got nigh onto twice as many men."

"Wholesale murder's pretty hard to cover up, Kell."

There was more at stake here than a bunch of cows, but Jackson would be damned if he'd spread his hand to this little weasel. Once he got the capital he needed from this raid, he'd dump Farley.

Jackson had his sights set on Hensen's whole outfit. The ranch sat on the Kaibab. Just east was a trail one of Farley's men told him about—a trail the man claimed to have run stolen horses over. The trail ran clear through the Grand Canyon.

From north to south rim the usual way was close to a 250 mile ride, most of it through or along the desert. But this horse thief trail Shesty told him about cut through the Canyon instead of around it, a distance of thirty miles! Jackson got excited just thinking about it.

North of Hensen, Mormon ranchers banded together to form the United Order or whatever the hell they called themselves, to protect their herds against rustlers.

Now if he could get his hands on the 3-H and work under the cloak of respectable rancher, he knew he could crack the Order. It was just one hell of a set-up for large-scale rustling operations between Utah and Arizona. But to make it work, he'd have to acquire Hensen's outfit without stirring up suspicions.

But that damn Farley! Jackson shook his head. Too much at stake here to let this runt foul things for him. Either he'd toe the mark or get shipped back to Nebraska.

Jackson dug into his pocket, pulled out an official looking paper and handed it to Farley.

Farley took the paper and examined it.

Farley looked back up at Jackson. "So what the hell is it?" Like most of his breed, Farley had never learned to read.

"It's a copy of your page in the *Wyoming Territorial Register of Convicts*. It says you were sent up eleven years ago when you were nineteen, for murdering a woman up there. You spent seven years at Laramie Prison then they transferred you to the Nebraska Pen. How come they sent you to Nebraska, Kell?"

Farley narrowed his eyes, wondering just what the hell Jackson was driving at. "It cost 60¢ a day to house prisoners at Nebraska, but a dollar back at Laramie. They shipped us lifers and hard-timers to Nebraska and damned if they didn't pocket the 40¢ difference themselves. Makes a fair sized bundle when you figger up the number of men they got out of their hair that way. So what about it?"

"Just wondering. It also says here you escaped from Nebraska a year ago April. You starting to get my drift now?"

At the little outlaw's blank look, Jackson cut it deeper.

"It means when *I* bark, *you* wag your tail or that damn tail will land right back in Nebraska."

Farley snorted and threw the paper on the ground.

"A piece of paper don't scare me, Jackson. Y'know, a bullet can shut anybody's mouth. Even yours."

"You want to try?"

Farley's hand snapped down. Before gunsight cleared leather he found himself slapped back against his horse, a Bowie against his throat. Farley breathed an obscenity.

A half-smile twisted Jackson's face as he applied the slightest pressure. "Understand this, you little bastard— I cut you into this deal. I can just as easy cut you out."

Jackson stepped back. "Now pick up that paper and hand it to me."

Farley's eyes spat hate. But as he fingered away the tiny beads of blood from his throat, he did as he was told.

"All right." Jackson smiled his dead smile, a smile that never reached his eyes. "Hensen's waiting for me and I've got to make tracks. But I got a job for you to take care of tonight . . . ."

IV

Josh Hensen's pacing flattened a circle in the snow. As Jackson approached, he yelled, "Where the hell you been! Find anything?"

Jackson took his time dismounting before answering. "Not much. You?"

With an impatient gesture, Hensen brushed Jackson's question aside. "Well, what'd you find?"

"Another small bunch run off . . . about a dozen head. Lost 'em in the squall."

Hensen jerked his hatbrim down further over his eyes, puffs of frost forming as he swore under his breath. "See who it was?"

Jackson shook his head. "But one of the horses pushing them had outsize tracks like that big geld Farley rides." He paused for dramatic effect. "The other set of tracks belonged to Walker. He might've been studying sign, same as me, but the ground was chewed up some . . . like restless horses might do while their riders set and jawed. " 'Course I can't be sure."

The hell you can't, Hensen thought. Jackson had wormed his way into the outfit, using the girls as a prod when he brought them here and he'd done nothing but stir up trouble ever since.

Walker on the other hand had been his *segundo* for a number of years. And for all his surly ways Bull Walker had always proved out dependable.

Of course that was before Walker married into the ranch by way of Libby. Could be he was getting big ideas . . . . Hensen's face creased into a frown.

22

Jackson, watching, smiled to himself. Shrewd enough not to push his remarks, he accomplished what he set out to do—tease Hensen into doubting his right-hand man.

Now, to strengthen the credibility of his report, Jackson added some straight goods.

"One other thing—on the way back I ran across the tracks of a rider with an unshod horse."

"The Paiute?" Hensen raised his eyebrows. He'd hired on the Indian as a tracker when the rustling got worse. But the damn 'breed was supposed to be up to Pipe Spring.

"Huh-uh, wasn't him. A white man leading his horse. I'd have to guess he's some down-to-his-blanket drifter out to bum a meal. His tracks headed flat and away toward the house."

Walker rode up in time to catch the tail end of Jackson's report.

"What's that?" Who's making tracks for the house?"

"Jackson figgers it's just some drifter."

"Then we'd better get our damn tails moving."

"What's the rush?"

"My gawd, Josh, what's the matter with you? You forgetting the women are there by theirselves?"

Jackson laughed. "What's the matter—ain't you man enough to hold your woman without you being on top of her every minute, Bull?" Jackson laid heavy emphasis on Walker's nickname.

"Why, damn you." Walker started out of his saddle.

Quickly Hensen raised a hand to restrain Bull and craned is neck around to face Jackson.

"Enough, you two. Time to be heading in anyway." He raised a palm skyward, indicating the new fall of snow beginning.

Lost in the drugged sleep of total exhaustion, Race's subconscious registered the return of Hensen and his crew, incorporating their sounds into his dreams.

Abruptly the dream shifted into a nightmare.

Race saw himself up on a sunfishing stud—17 hands of twisting red hell. The bronc swapped ends, crashing

*against the corral bars. Air whooshed out of Race's lungs
as he slammed against the top rail. The leg crushed
between horse and post, but it was his ribs that felt broke.*

Dammit, hold on! Can't—I'm trying!

*Each wild jump drove the cracked ribs further into his
muscles. Another frenzied snap and Race jetted
backwards over the stud's muscled rump.*

*Race hung fire, crazily suspended in mid-air, above the
horse. With exaggerated slowness the stud's steel-clad
hooves climbed steadily to that moment of exploding
impact.*

Race bolted upright, a ragged pain tearing at his ribs. A
bull's-eye lantern trained on his face momentarily blinded
him. Twisting away from the glare, he caught the blur of a
cocked boot hurtling toward him.

Race balled up to protect the vital spots, but a hand
fastened in his hair, lifting him. Hampered by sleep-
drugged reflexes and the unyielding knee, Race was carried
forward by his own momentum. He crashed face-first into
the raw boards of the loft.

Stunned, he shook his head to clear it. Through a
reddish haze he saw two men. One, holding the lantern,
stood on the ladder, his armpits level with the loft floor.
The other, built like a bull buffalo, stood alongside Race.
The big man's leg was drawn back ready to take another
swipe at Race.

"That's enough, Bull." The man on the ladder climbed
the rest of the way up onto the loft and nudged Race with
his foot. A cutaway holster hung from this man's hips,
clearly marking his calling. "He's awake now, Bull. Better
watch it. He might take a notion to hit back."

His tone carried more taunt than warning.

"Damn you, Jackson, you figgering to take up for this
bum?"

Jackson shrugged. He didn't give a damn one way or the
other if Bull kicked the drifter's head off. It was just too
good an opportunity to get some digs in at Walker.

Temporarily forgotten by the other two, Race took hold
of an upright and after he struggled to his feet leaned
against it, trying to clear the sleepfog from his brain. He

24

gasped air into his heaving lungs, rubbing the bruised ribs.

He wondered who the hell these two were. The yellow-haired gunman was sure enough baiting the bronc who did the boot work. Race watched.

"What d'you mean?" Bull aped Jackson's shrug. His eyes narrowed in suspicion. "Come to think of it, how were you so damn sure somebody was here the minute we stepped into the barn?"

Jackson's lips pulled back from his teeth in what passed for a smile. "I just have more damn brains than you."

To a man like Jackson, keenness to detail meant survival. The moment they entered the barn, he sensed something out of kilter. Pressed, he couldn't have told exactly what it was. An extra sound. The smell of wet wool. Little things that belonged after they settled in, not before.

"More damn brains, hell! Maybe you can pull that crap on Josh, but I've got you pegged, Jackson. And you come out smelling worse than last week's dung heap."

Jackson's smile evaporated, along with his mocking nonchalance. He turned his body slightly, right hand brushing leather, his whole posture challenging.

Bull swallowed noisily. He had guts enough and he'd meet Jackson head-on any day of the week—but not with guns. He couldn't begin to match cutters with that gunnie and he knew it.

"Say, what the hell's goin' on up there anyway?" Hensen's voice grated impatiently from below. "You found someone up there, bring him down. Bandy, get another lamp going here, will you?"

As tension released between Maize Jackson and Bull Walker, attention reverted to the cowboy. Venting his frustrated rage on Race, Bull dug his heavy fingers into his shoulder and spun him away from the upright. Before Race could catch his balance, Walker set his booted foot against the cowboy's spine and shoved.

Race sprawled forward, claying at the support timber, the only thing that kept him from taking a header into one of the stalls below.

That tied it!

Mad as hell with the hide off, Race sprang to his feet and lunged for Walker. He didn't know what kind of tough lay he'd bungled into, and the shape he was in, he was likely to take a hell of a beating. But it would be worth it just to get in a few good licks at this soft-bellied son.

Race's skull pile-drove right into Bull's unprotected midriff. Bull doubled over, clutching his stomach. While Bull was still bent over, Race sliced his interlocked fists upward, catching the heavier man solidly under the jaw. Walker's neck snapped back and Race hoped he broke it. That shot about took up the last of his strength. Too exhausted to follow through, Race stood there raking in great gulps of air.

The *segundo* gathered himself and rose to his feet, watching Race. Slowly a grin of understanding spread across his face.

Grimly reading the other's expression, Race thought, *Here's where I get mine. But damned if I'll roll over and play dead.*

Tucking his chin against his chest, Race moved in to meet his bulky opponent as the other charged forward.

Jackson yelled, "Hold it!"

Like a finger-snap a gun appeared in his hand. Both men stopped dead, not certain which of them he'd use it on. Raw hate flared in Bull's eyes as he looked first one man to the other. The blood still pounded in Race's ears, not quite willing to drop this dogfight himself. But reason told him Jackson's intervention was saving him from a hell of a beating.

Pointing with the barrel of his gun, Jackson ordered, "Get the hell down there. Bull, you first."

Bull looked at each of them again, nodded as if to himself. Then he said to Race, "We ain't through. We'll finish sometime when your wet nurse ain't handy."

The three climbed down the ladder, Race bookended by the two 3-H men. Down on the dirt-packed floor, Jackson herded Race toward a thickset man of middle-age. The only thing remarkable about the man was the sour expression on his face.

Ignoring Race, he spoke to Jackson. "Check him for hardware?"

Maine nodded. "Slick as a new-dropped calf."

Only then did the older man turn to Race.

"Okay, bum, you got a name?"

Race was tempted to tell him to go to hell, but common sense ruled. Might as well charge Hell with a bucket of water as buck this snake-bit crew.

"The name's Evans . . . Race Evans."

"Ah-huh. And what's your summer name?"

That kind of question was more than a breach of range etiquette. It was a deliberate insult, implying that Race was on the dodge. Race's face hardened. Soft answers wouldn't curry favor with this outfit. He was in for hell regardless, so he answered accordingly.

"Unless you're Josh Hensen, I don't guess that's any of your damn business."

"I am Hensen."

Race's eyes flicked over the stocky man in surprise. He thought sure the girl said Hensen was her brother. But this man, calf-legged and ugly as a bar of homemade soap, no way resembled the girl who'd braced him earlier. Moreover, this man was easily twenty, twenty-five years her senior.

Hensen interrupted his thoughts. "Look here, bum, you got a reason for being here, I want to hear it. And it better be a damn good one."

"I was waiting for you."

"So?"

"I'm hunting up a berth."

"Well, you ain't got one here. What the hell gave you the idea you could come in here, help yourself to a stall for that nag, and use my barn for a flop-house!"

"The lady told me I could wait here for you."

"Oh, sure. What lady?"

"How'n hell am I supposed to know! She told me Josh Hensen was her brother and I could wait for him here."

"You're a goddamn liar!"

Ordinarily Race was easygoing, but Hensen was putting

27

the spurs to him pretty good and that was the second time today he'd been called that. Automatically his fists balled and, the cords standing out in his neck, he took a step toward Hensen.

"Huh-uh," came from his side. Jackson again, his hand lightly tapping the holstered gun at his side.

Race stopped, swearing in frustration.

"I'll say it again," said Hensen. "You're a goddamn liar. Every person on this ranch has strict orders to run off any strangers. An' here you're telling me my own sister welcomed you with open arms, told you to make yourself right to home. Maybe she even invited you up to the house for tea, huh?"

"I didn't say that." The words gritted out.

"Well, whatever your story is, make it good 'cause I'm anxious to hear it."

"When I rode up, a young lady braced me, told me to head out. After some talk, I made to go. But she changed her mind then and let me wait for you in here. For God's sake you saw the doors were locked from the outside."

Hensen thought on that a minute. "Why'd she change her mind?"

"How the hell should I know."

"All right. Lin, fetch Sage here. Pronto!" He looked at Race. "You can repeat that cock-and-bull story in front of my sister, because I'm sure as hell not buying it." Then he muttered just loud enough for Race to hear, "If she did let you stay, I'll strip the hide off her goddamn back."

That stopped Race cold. When he had asked the girl to let him wait, it never occurred to him she might be letting herself in for trouble with her own brother. But from what he'd seen of Hensen and this crew, he believed the man capable of doing just what he promised. That decided Race.

"All right, Hensen. You called my bluff. No need to call the girl or anyone else down here. I lied. The girl run me off with a shotgun but I snuck back. I was in a bad way and like I said, looking for a winter berth. If you can't use me, I'll collect my gear and shag out of here."

"The hell you will." Without warning, Hensen drove his

28

fist into Race's face. Thunder roared and lightening flashed inside his skull as he whiplashed against the end stall. Blood gushed from his nose and blistered mouth.

Normally, a lean hundred seventy-five pounds covered Race's six-foot-two-inch frame, but he'd dropped a good thirty pounds since he'd gotten his walking papers from Swan. He wasn't about to take a pounding if he could help it. He grabbed a broken singletree that was hanging from one of the support posts and squared around in a batting crouch.

"All right, you bastard, you want it, just come and get it!"

"No! Stop it!" Sage's frightened scream overlaid Race's challenge. She rushed forward, Lin at her heels. When she saw Race's bloody face, she stopped short. Sickened by the sight, she whirled to face her brother.

"Josh, what's going on?"

"This damn drifter you run off snuck back here. I've just been making sure he stays run off this time."

"What do you mean sneaked back? I told . . ."

"This don't concern you, Miss." Race cut her off before she could contradict what he said. No use both of them taking the stick. "Why don't you just head back to the house where you belong."

Sage spared Race an annoyed glance. "I don't know what's been said or done here or what he told you, Josh. But I told him he could wait in here for you."

"You what! Why, for God's sake?"

"Have you seen his horse? With the storm and all . . ." she shook her head. "Besides, I made sure he wasn't armed."

"Well now," Hensen broke in, "you see what he's got in his hands? Whether you get your brains blowed out or knocked out, you're just as dead!"

Race still held the singletree cocked and ready to swing.

Hensen grabbed Sage by the wrist, twisted her to face Race. "You don't need a gun to bash out somebody's brains. By God, I've got half a mind to . . ."

"Dammit, let her alone! Stop faulting the lady for a show of decency. You gotta vent your spleen on somebody, then c'mon finish with me." Race motioned Hensen to him with one hand.

"Keep outa this, bum! What'd you want to lie for in the first place."

"I told you straight. It wasn't till you got so free with threats on your sister that I changed my story."

Sage stared at Race, a look of puzzlement fading into one of grudging respect.

Hensen looked at him, too, then at Sage. Then, as if he just remembered them, he looked at his crew standing around. Lin and Bandy dropped their heads, embarrassed at what they were witnessing. Jackson stood back in the shadows, but Hensen had no doubt whose part the man would take if it came down to "choosers" between Sage and him. He was sure only of Walker and Keno. *Or was he*? Discretion dictated a little backtracking here.

Rubbing a thorny hand across his forehead, Hensen said, "This trouble with Farley's got me walkin' on eggs. It's just that none of this trouble really started until . . . aw, hell!"

"Until I came to live with you," Sage finished for him.

"Those are your words, not mine," he said and stomped out.

The rest filed out after him, carrying the lanterns. Standing alone in the darkness, Race slowly lowered the singletree, feeling a little weak in the knees. He let his breath out suddenly, swore when he realized he'd been holding it.

He let the singletree drop and wobbled to the doors, feeling like he'd been run through a meat chopper. The doors weren't locked this time and he stepped through. It was still snowing but not as hard.

Race scooped up a handful of the clean snow and held its soothing coolness against his battered lips. He rubbed his face clean, spit out the blood, and let another handful of snow melt inside his mouth. His teeth hurt clear down to the roots, but the cold numbed his lips and would keep the swelling down.

Race flinched as someone grabbed his arm. Somehow Jackson had slipped back on him.

30

"Easy, drifter. It's just me. Boss says you're to come up on to the house for a feed."

Race paused. "I'm not looking for a handout. I need a job."

"Suit yourself. But pride don't fill an empty belly. You can talk job on a full stomach as well as an empty one," and he turned and walked away.

The dark and snow swallowed Jackson up. With a shrug, Race dabbed gingerly at his face with a soiled kerchief. Other than that there wasn't all that much he could do about his appearance. Dirty and travel-worn as they were, the clothes on his back were all he had. He beat at them some with his hat, then tried to punch the hat back into some semblance of shape. Before clamping the broad-rimmed woolsey back on his head, he ran his fingers through his hair by way of combing it.

Race struck the drift fence and followed it until he caught the orange halo of light from the ranchhouse's front window.

As he reached the steps, he saw Bull Walker and Maize Jackson, vague shapes arguing on the porch. Neither man seemed aware of Race, or if they were, they ignored him.

Walker had a hand against Jackson's chest. "Just what business did you have with that bum?"

"My business." He pushed Bull's hand aside.

"Listen, damn you, as long as you're on 3-H, you'll take orders from me. You have too free a way of forgetting I'm more than *segundo* around here. I have a share in this outfit same as Josh and Sage."

"You have crap. So long as Libby's alive you got nothing. And anytime you think you're boss, just try firing me. So there's no mistakin', Bull, I got only one boss and it sure as Christ ain't you." Jackson shouldered past Walker into the house.

Bull glared after him, hesitated a few moments, then followed. Race considered what he overheard. The Hensen girl wasn't just making squaw talk when she said this outfit had troubles enough of its own.

If he had any other alternative, Race would shake the

dust of this outfit *muy pronto*. With wry humor he reminded himself of the old saw: Beggars can't be choosers.

Feeling jaded as a whore on a Saturday night, Race mounted the porch.

V

In answer to Race's knock, a withered old Mexican opened the door. The *viejo* screwed up his face and with a deliberate show of reluctance let Race in. Then without so much as a "kiss my foot" the old man padded away, leaving Race to stand awkwardly just inside the door.

The steamy pungence of cooking food hit the cowboy all at once. He had to swallow hard and repeatedly to keep down the sudden rush of nausea. Damn, it'd been too long since he'd put away an honest-to-god meal.

At that moment, Sage and a handsome woman of about thirty-five entered the kitchen area. A little belatedly Race remembered to draw off his hat. The Mexican passed by the two women muttering loud enough for Race to hear: "*El señor deberia comer con los marranos.*"

Texan by birth, Race knew enough border Spanish to translate roughly. Boiled down, the old man said Race was fit to eat with the pigs.

Sage briefly took aside the old man she called "Haysoos." Meanwhile the other woman walked over to Race and introduced herself.

"I'm Libby Walker."

A little self-consciously Race took her extended hand. "Race Evans, ma'am."

When Sage joined them, Libby excused herself to help Jésus. Sage's gaze settled on Race's blistered mouth, half-regretting her impulse that sent Jackson to bring the drifter up to the house for supper. Much of what ran through her mind showed on her face and Race was perceptive enough to catch it.

33

He said, "The *viejo* was right. I'm awful dirty."

"Oh. I'm sorry you understood what Jésus said."

The way she said it made clear she wasn't sorry for what the old man said—only that Race understood it. Race passed it off with an embarrassed shrug.

"If there's some place I can clean up . . ."

Sage nodded. "Jésus, call Jackson out here, please."

The old man went through the doorway off the far right end of the kitchen. Shortly after, Maize came ambling out.

What a contrast between him and the drifter, Sage thought. Jackson's person, his clothes were immaculate. Polished boots reflected the lantern light. The only crease in his striped trousers was the one that belonged there.

There were other differences, too. Although both men were nearly of a height, Jackson outweighed the other by a solid fifty pounds. Sage had to admit Race looked like he hadn't been eating too regularly. Gaunt hollows shadowed-under his eyes and cheekbones.

Since she hadn't been able to make out his face earlier, she looked closely now. Like Jackson, he had blue eyes. But while Jackson's resembled pieces of chipped ice, the drifter's were hotly alive, like molten cobalt, if there were such a thing. Both had light hair, too. Maize favored his thinning yellow hair by combing it carefully to one side. Not that Jackson was all that old—about the same age as Libby.

On the other hand, Race looked younger than Sage first thought, maybe his late twenties or early thirties. And the cowboy's shaggy mane of sand-colored hair, like his darkly contrasting skin, were byproducts of countless hours spent working in the out-of-doors.

The long blunt-tipped fingers that fiddled with the beaten sombrero bore rope scars and callouses. Sage thought of Jackson's well-manicured hands. She knew for a fact that Jackson shunned manual labor like a paycar shuns a hobo.

Impatience stirred Sage as she realized Jackson, rather than the drifter, was suffering by the comparison.

Abruptly she ordered Maize, "Show the drifter—I mean Mr. Evans where he can clean up."

With a mock salute to Sage, Jackson motioned Race to follow him. Race learned the narrow room elling off the log kitchen housed the cowboys. They didn't have a separate bunkhouse.

Voices drifted to him through the closed door. But the minute they opened the door whatever good-natured wrangling had been going on stopped dead.

Jackson pointed to a cracked porcelain bowl with gray water standing in it. Above, on a roller, hung a much-used community towel.

Race didn't care. Even the eye-stinging bite of the lye soap on his cuts felt good. Soap, like so many other things, was a luxury he had done without the past several weeks. He rubbed a hand over his matted whiskers. He'd like to shave, but a reluctant pride kept him from asking Jackson the use of a razor.

After the other hands drifted out, Race asked, "Jackson, you figure any chance of Hensen taking me on?"

The yellow-haired man shrugged. "Can't say you exactly made a hit with the old man. Hard telling, though. Trouble he's been having—or claims to be having—he might figure to take on an extra hand."

"I got a letter of recommend from my last boss."

"Could help, but with him, aint no telling."

"Miss Hensen mentioned you all've been having trouble?"

"Rustling, mostly."

"How about other outfits around here?"

Jackson shook his head.

"What did Miss Hensen mean about the trouble starting after she got here—if you don't mind talking about it."

Jackson didn't mind. Always one to copper his bets, he welcomed any chance to cast his poison seeds, to weaken Hensen's hand any way he could while strengthening his own.

"Aw, that's crap. Farley'd been living off 3-H stuff all last year from what Keno told me. Hell, I just brought Sage and Libby here a couple months ago. Hensen's just got his nose out of joint 'cause their old man cut in the girls for equal shares on this outfit. Sage is just his half-sister and Libby ain't even related.

"Way I understand it, when Hensen was already full-grown and rodding this outfit, his old man up and married a circuit preacher's daughter. He got religion himself and hit the glory trail, leaving Josh to run this place.

"After Sage was born, she traveled with her parents till she got old enough to teach at their church's mission school. Libby was Mrs. Hensen's niece and went to work with them after her husband died. Met Lib this summer. She found me bad hurt and nursed me through.

"Once I got back on my feet, I kinda hung on, thinking I owed 'em. Turned out to be a good thing for both Libby and Sage I did. One day when Lib and I went in town for supplies, we come back the next day to camp and found the Hensens dead. Best we could figure, renegades hit 'em sometime during the night.

"While we were sorting through the wreckage, I found a paper, like a will, naming the girls owners even-up with Josh on this outfit—and I mean on everything, from bedstraw to bottomland. Me and Lib salvaged what we could, gathered up Sage from the school and came on here.

"Hensen wasn't putting out no welcome signs, and if I hadn't been along, I doubt the girls could've made their claims stick. Talking about this trouble makes me wonder sometimes if Hensen aint behind this trouble himself, just to scare off the women."

Race thought about what Jackson told him, but offered no comment. The gunman gave him a hell of a lot more information than he asked for and he couldn't help but wonder why.

He shrugged it off. Unless he got a job here, it was none of his damn business one way or the other.

VI

Iron clacked dully on iron, followed by the Mexican's call to supper.

Maize led off through the bunkroom across the kitchen to a wide doorway leading to the clapboard-covered part of the house.

Race examined the large living quarters with more than idle curiosity—with an outfit as ringey as this one, no telling when he might need to exit the quickest way possible.

When Hensen came down from upstairs by way of the living room staircase into the dining area, he saw Race. His head twisted in surprise, his lips tightened as if to say something. Instead, he took his seat at the head of the table, looking like he'd been weaned on curdled milk.

Race assumed from Hensen's reaction that he wasn't the one who sent Jackson to fetch him up to the house. And it sure as hell wasn't Bull Walker. That meant one of two things—either Jackson acted on his own hook, or one of the women sent him, probably the girl. Race preferred to think it was the latter, and a little surge of pleasure stirred him.

The others were already seated around the table, Walker, Keno and Bandy taking up the left bench, Lin on the right side, next to Hensen.

Jackson corked a thumb, telling Race, "Have a seat."

But Race didn't intend to get himself hamstrung between two 3-H men. He held up his left hand and told Jackson, "I feed from the near side. If it's all the same to you, I'll just ride this end of the bench. Save us getting our elbows knotted."

Jackson hesitated, a look of shrewd appraisal on his face, before he finally nodded, "Why sure, cowboy."

The seat Race chose, while not the most comfortable was the safest. It meant straddling the broad table leg since he couldn't bend his left leg around it.

Eager to dig in, Race wondered what the holdup was when the two women took up the chairs at the end beside him. No place he ever worked did the womenfolk sit down to eat with the hired hands.

Suddenly he became painfully aware of his appearance. The way Bandy and Jackson and the others were slicked up, he should have guessed. Even if he had known, there wasn't that much he could do, except maybe leave his jacket on, for his clothes verged on the indecent.

The snaps were all torn off his shirt, exposing his faded flannel undershirt. Sleeves were still rolled up, too, from when he washed. Self-consciously he let down one sleeve. The way it hung in tatters, Race decided looked even worse, so he hurriedly rolled it back up above his elbow.

He caught Sage watching him but nobody else seemed to pay particular notice. And once Libby turned thanks, the signal for Jésus to begin carting out the food, Race forgot about it himself.

Slabs of roast beef filled platters at each end of the table, along with bowls of gravy, hot biscuits, stewed tomatoes, creamed corn, fried apples, coffee and tea, and dried apricot pies. A cowboy's dream!

Race's stomach tightened fiercely at sight of all that food. Meals had been too few and too irregular in recent weeks. To keep each bite from coming back up, Race had to wash it down with several gulps of coffee. Having access to all this food but being unable to eat it filled the cowboy with a peculiar frustation bordering on anger.

From where she sat at a right angle to Race's left elbow, Sage put another interpretation on the way he toyed with his food. So far as she was concerned, it confirmed her earlier suspicions of him. Just after a normal day's work on the range, the other men were wolfing down their food. True, the drifter's gaunt appearance had fooled her at first. But that was probably the reason Farley sent him instead of someone else.

Disgusted at being taken in, Sage in a huff jerked her chair closer to the table only to bump smack up against Race's game leg.

With all the room he had on his side of the table, why did he have to crowd her at her end! She poked lightly at his foot with her toe, hoping he'd be gentleman enough to take the hint and pull his leg around on his side of the table leg where it belonged. When he ignored the hint, Sage in anger drew her foot back and kicked his ankle sharply.

"Umhh!" Race grunted wondering what the hell that was about. He shot a burning glance across the table at Walker. *If that dirty son was trying to hooraw him . . .*

But the bulky *segundo* was in another world, shoveling the food in as fast as his mouth could take it.

Then dammit, who? Puzzled, Race turned to look at Sage. As he stared at her, color rose high on her cheeks and her shoulder dipped as he felt another solid thud to his ankle.

What the hell, he wondered, *is she mad about?* Shifting his weight to the back of the bench, he glimpsed under the table. Nothing there but his leg stacked snug against hers.

For God's sake! Sure she doesn't think I'm trying . . . Color rose about his frazzled collar. He didn't know how to begin to explain.

Oh hell. Why should I even try. Dropping his glance, he focused his eyes on his plate.

"Mr. Evans." The words came distinctly and loud enough for everyone to hear. He didn't look up. Until now the byplay between him and Sage had gone unnoticed. But if she chose to call attention to it . . . . With a weary sigh, he laid down his fork and looked at Sage.

"Yoo-hoo—over here." Libby wriggled her fingers at him, smiling. It was she who had spoken. "Looks like you're having trouble eating. After supper why don't you let Jésus give you some spirits of camphor to put on those cold sores. It'll ease the tenderness and help dry them."

Relieved, Race returned her smile. "Thank you, ma'am.

39

That's real kind." Walker looked sharply at Race, frowning.

Now what!

He was about ready to give up trying to figure out the people around here, when he remembered Libby was Bull's wife. Now that was a real mismatch!

Another painful thunk to his shinbone yanked Race back to earth.

"Look," he said to Sage in a quiet but distinctly pronounced drawl, "you're not a bad-looking girl, but I've seen plenty better." That wasn't exactly the truth, but he'd about had it with her orneriness. Since he'd eaten about all he could safely handle anyway, he said, "If you'll give me some clearance, I'll get the hell out of your way."

"Your language is as inexcusable as your behavior," she returned as quietly, then added, ". . . but you are the first cowboy I've ever seen who couldn't make a simple dismount from a table bench without asking a lady's help."

A shadow crossed Race's face. For such a pretty little thing, she sure knew how to poke at the tender spots. That crippled leg had not only cost him the few extra dollars he earned for riding the rough string, but had cost him the job itself.

If a puncher had made the remark she just did, he'd have busted him wide open. But what could he do to her? In all his life this had to be the most frustrating meal he had ever sat down to, and of the few women he had known, Sage Hensen had to be the most aggravating.

With an upward tilt of her chin, Sage slid her chair back to permit him exit, effectively dismissing him. Race slid off the end of the bench and went directly into the kitchen, not knowing what the others at the table might be thinking, and not giving a damn.

In the kitchen, Jésus was only about half through his own meal, so Race started scrubbing on the pans. At least he'd pay for what he ate. He didn't want to owe any damn one of this outfit any damn thing.

By the time supper ended, Jésus had thawed some

toward Race and Race had simmered down himself. When Sage and Libby, arms full of dirty dishes, joined them, Race had already applied the camphor and the two men were deep in a discussion of the relative merits of hemp lariats versus the rawhide reatas.

First chance he got, Race approached Sage. Hesitantly he asked, "Could I have a minute with you?" She ignored him and walked away.

A little later he tried again. And again. The last time, she spun to face him. "Why don't you just quit!"

"I can't, ma'am," he grinned. "I'm like a steer—I just naturally have to keep on trying."

The words just kind of sneaked out and Race immediately bit his tongue. Damn, he'd have to remember to curb that corral talk around the ladies.

Torn between indignation and curiosity, Sage asked, "Just what is it you want anyway?"

"First off, I've been wanting to apologize for getting you into trouble with your brother."

She lifted her shoulders as if it were unimportant.

"I'm sorry about at the supper table, too, though you're wrong about that." Race lifted a hand bebfore she had a chance to argue the point. "What I mean is it wasn't what you thought it was and I got sure enough mad." If Sage had been a little more receptive to his apologies, he would have explained about his knee-joint being froze.

As it was, she was pretty hostile and he really couldn't understand it. He had something else to ask her, but now he hesitated.

"If you're through . . ." she started to turn away.

"No, ma'am." His pride had already taken a hell of a walloping—one more time wouldn't make that much of a difference. Race plunged head first into icy waters.

"I've got a favor to ask of you. Jésus said you don't ordinarily save the leftovers. He said it's okay by him, but for me to check with you first . . . could I hold out some of the left-over chuck?"

"For what?"

"Why, for me to eat later. Since you throw it away any-

41

how, I thought maybe . . ."

"No." Anger shaped Sage's answer as she remembered the way he had trifled with his meal. "Table scraps go to the dog. I throw out what's left when *he's* through."

A brief fire flared in Race's eyes, faded almost as quickly into dispassionate acceptance. Rubbing salt into the wound, Race ended up having to cart the kettle of scraps out to the dog himself.

As the dog wolfed the food, Race broke into a mirthless grin.

"The lady said to feed the dog and by her lights I'm a sure-enough son-of-a-bitch . . ." and he grabbed a hunk of beef away from the hound and crammed it into his coat pocket.

VII

When Race returned to the house, Jackson was waiting.

"Hensen'll talk to you whenever you finish up in here."

"About done now." Race set down the empty kettle, draped his jacket over one of the kitchen chairs and followed Jackson into the big room. As best he could, Race minimized his limp.

It wasn't all that noticeable, but he was getting a mite sensitive about it, knowing full well it didn't help his chances any of nailing down a job.

Race hoped to talk to Hensen alone. Disappointed, he noted that except for Jésus, the whole damn crew appeared to be stacked around the room: Sage in the corner rocker by the fireplace, Hensen and Libby on the leather settee in front of it, Walker and the other cowboys around the deal table, playing penny ante.

Jackson split away from Race to join the other hands at the round table. Only Walker declined Jackson's challenge to a game of freezeout. That sharper had taken him too many times. Bull enjoyed an occasional game of straight draw or stud, but he didn't like the restrictions of freezeout. You couldn't add to your original table stakes or draw down from them or from your winnings. You just had to play until you won everybody else's stake or until you lost your own. In freezeout there could be only one winner and too often that winner was Jackson.

He rose from the table and sat down on the settee between Hensen and Libby.

"Just as well," Jackson remarked to the others. "Never knowed scared money to win nohow."

With a disgusted snort, Bull left his wife and rejoined the other men. Maize stifled a smile and in that instant Race understood that Jackson was a man who derived as much pleasure from manipulating people as he did the pasteboards.

Race hung back, watching the byplay, still hoping for a private palaver with the boss. But the rancher, busy cleaning the shotgun Sage had fired earlier, called him over with an impatient jerk of the head.

As Race stepped between Hensen and Sage, the latter pointedly ignored him. Her attitude drew a pang. All curled up that way in the rocker, a basket of mending on her lap, the fire's shadows playing across her features, Sage made a picture that represented all Race had ever hoped for—a place of his own and a good woman to share it with.

With a shrug he jammed his hands down into the hip pockets of his Levi's and squared to face the rancher.

"You claim to be lookin' for work, Evans?"

"I am looking for work."

"Uh-huh. Well, unless you got something special to offer, I don't see no reason for taking another rider on. Got more'n I need now to carry over the winter."

"It don't have to be riding special, Mr. Hensen."

"How's that?"

Without saying it in so many words, he had to let Hensen know just how desperate he was to tie on with an outfit. Up to now he'd had the same independent pride as any other cowpuncher that kept him a notch above what they considered common laborers. If a job couldn't be done horseback, it wasn't worth doing. He'd known more than one puncher to quit an outfit rather than tackle the blister end of a shovel.

He chose his words carefully to get his point across.

"I make a pretty good hand with tools and such. C'n mend harness, work leather, carpenter, chop wood, string wire . . . dig post holes if that's what needs doing."

Hensen cocked an eyebrow at the cowboy. He got the message.

"Where'd you work last?"

"Swan up on the Chugwater for the last three years. Busted broncs during the winter, rode the rough-string the rest of the time."

"Swan. That's one of them big foreign syndicates up in Wyoming, ain't it?" At Race's nod, Hensen probed, "Understand those outfits been havin' trouble with their own punchers mavericking company steers. That have anything to do with your leaving?"

"No." He bit the word short against a stir of resentment. He was meeting Hensen now as job hunter to prospective boss and he had to walk light.

"I was a bronc peeler till a hammerhead unloaded me. Busted me up pretty good. By the time the doc got through piecing me back together, the bottom fell out of the market and there was a dozen men fighting for every open job.

"Big outfit like Swan draws top riders under any conditions. When I was able to get back to work, the range boss of our section told me he couldn't use me no more. He wrote me up a letter of recommend and sent me packing."

"For someone who's been workin' steady for three years, you ain't got much of an outfit."

"That's so. Sold or traded off my outfit, first to pay off the doc, then later for grub for me or feed for the mare . . . been close to three months since I've drawed a pay."

"Uh-huh. You still got that letter your boss wrote for you?"

"You bet." Race dipped two long blunt fingers into the match pocket of his jeans and dug out a creased sheet of brown paper. His hand shook a little as he held the note out to Hensen, his muscles tense. He'd just about given up hope of landing a berth anywhere, least of all here. But from the way Hensen was talking . . .

Hands grimed with gunslick, Josh motioned Race to hand the letter to Sage. "Let her read it."

Without looking up at him, she accepted the letter,

quickly scanned it. Hensen chafed at the bit. "Well, go on, read it out loud. What're you waitin' on?"

Ignoring Josh, Sage looked directly at Race for the first time since he entered the room. "Mr. Evans, do you want this letter read aloud?"

"Why sure, yes, ma'am."

She seemed surprised. "All of it?"

The way she asked set up a sudden rush of doubt in Race. It also caught the interest of the rest of the people in the room. Stirring uneasily he said, "Yes, go ahead."

Sage read aloud, deciphering the crudely printed note:

Sep 1886

The bearer of this note is one Race Evans. He's a willing worker and made top hand till he got busted up. He worked for Swan about three years, ever since he got let out of the Territorial Pen up to Laramie.

Yrs truly
Roy Singhaus
Swan Land & Cattle Co
Wyoming Territory

Race's insides turned to ice water. He heard a little gasp of shock from Libby off to his left. Hell, what Singhaus put in that letter was as much a surprise to him as anyone else in that room. Forcing all expression from his face, he watched Hensen, trying to read the boss' reaction.

Across the room, Walker jeered aloud, "Well, now. A *tiger*."

"Hobble your lip, Bull." Hensen shut-off the *segundo*. Then to Race, "How long were you in?"

Race flashed a look in Sage's direction before answering, "Seven years."

"For what?"

"Involuntary manslaughter."

"Seven years is a long go for involuntary . . . what you holdin' back?"

Race hesitated. But as long as there was still an off-chance of being hired on, he'd better answer all of Hensen's questions straight. He just wished to God the women weren't hearing all this.

46

"The law gave me eight years for manslaughter and cattle rustling. Knocked almost a year off for 'good time.' "

"Uh-huh. Now that's something." Hensen rubbed his hand across his forehead, thinking. He wanted to talk some more to this drifter, but not here, not with everybody all ears.

"Tell you what, Evans, I'll need to think on this a little bit. Like I said, we're pretty full up. You wait for me down to the barn. I'll join you later, tell you then what I've decided."

"Sure. You bet." But Race knew he didn't stand a chance in hell of catching a berth with this outfit now. Sick with shame and disappointment, he couldn't face the women as he murmured a hurried thanks for the meal and shagged out of there.

Jackson pushed his remaining table stakes into the pot, folded his cards and followed Race. He caught him at the door.

The drifter genuinely had him stumped and he said so. "After what I told you tonight about Hensen's trouble—the rustling and all—how the hell'd you figure that letter to help you any?"

Race shook his head. "I didn't know what was in it."

"Aw, c'mon. Carrying that thing around for what—three months? And you never read it?"

"If I knew what was in it, do you think I'd've flashed the damn thing around every outfit between here and the Chug! Hell! I can't read."

Shaking his head in disgust, Race crushed his shapeless hat to his head and stormed out into the night.

VIII

Josh Hensen considered the situation at 3-H. Things were going to hell in a basket what with one thing then another. Seemed everybody and his uncle wanted a piece of his ranch. It belonged to him by all rights and he damn well intended to keep it that way. If the ex-con would go along with him—and Hensen had no reason to expect he wouldn't—he could make use of the man.

"Did you hear me, Josh?" Walker's coarse voice intruded on the rancher's thoughts. "I say we run that damn jailbird over the hill tonight."

"It aint your say-so, Bull."

"The hell it ain't. I'm thinking about the women."

Jackson, again back at the deal table laughed. "Hell, man. Anything in pants gets within roping distance of your wife you take fits."

"Yeah, well I'm thinking of Sage as much as Libby. Them jailbirds are all alike. Locked up away from women so long, once they're set loose they can't control themselves. Sure, right now all he's got his mind set on is filling his empty gut and throwing his bedroll in a dry corner. But once that's taken care of, it'll be the woman-hunger that tiger'll want to satisfy. Mark my words."

In the past, Sage had always made a point of keeping her nose out of the men's discussions. But Bull's reasoning struck her as so absurd, she spoke out.

"The man's been out of prison for three years. If he wanted to take advantage of a woman, he had all the

48

opportunity in the world this afternoon . . . and don't say it's because he was too worried about his next meal. I watched him at supper tonight. He barely ate half as much as I did.''

"Little lady, if you don't know any more'n that about a man's natural hungers—food or women—you got some mighty hard lessons ahead of you. That tiger's half-starved to death—both ways, you can bet!''

"All this gab is beside the point," Hensen interrupted. "The point is that no matter who says what, I'm still running this outfit and I'll decide whether the drifter goes or stays.''

All hope washed out of him, Race sat on an inverted keg just inside the barn. When Hensen slipped through one of the doors, he nearly tripped over Race in the darkness.

Raising his bull's-eye lantern he said, "Evans? Why the hell you sitting in the dark?''

Race just shrugged. He didn't even have any matches. Hensen lifted down a lantern from a nail, lit it, then tossed the remaining "stinkers" on the block to Race. Race caught the sulfur matches and with a nod of thanks dropped them into his shirt pocket. Then he settled down to wait for Hensen to speak, certain what the big augur would say and not all-fired anxious to hear it.

Finally Hensen took the bit. "All things considered, I don't see that I can take you as a regular, Evans. This is a small outfit. Ordinarily I wouldn't be wintering as big a crew as I have right now if it wasn't for this trouble with Farley. Ready cash is another problem. Not even a place for you to stay, with the bunks full up to the house.''

"Sure, I understand," Race said, unable to keep a tinge of bitterness out of his voice.

"Huh-uh, Evans," Hensen spoke mildly. "Ain't necessarily what you're thinking. Want you to know I appreciate your being honest with me about being in prison.''

"Honest, hell!" Race shivered then, as much from emotion as the cold. His eyes held the rancher's in the flickering lamplight. "Being in the pen isn't something a man brags on. If I'd knowed what Singhaus put in that letter, I'd have burned the damned thing!"

"Look, Hensen," he said earnestly, "if there's any way you can see your way clear to take me on—maybe just for a week."

Seeing the refusal build on Hensen's lips, he hurried on. "I'm not asking wages . . . just a few days' rest and feed for the mare and me. I can bed down right here. Plenty odd jobs around here need doing. And whatever dust is on my backtrail, I never yet shied a man on a full day's work. Any job you set me to, I'll do it and I'll do it right."

Hensen bowed his head, rubbed his face to conceal the satisfaction Race's last words brought him. "So you'd do any job? How about something along your old line of work . . . and I'm not referring to snapping broncs."

The double-faced question drew Race up short. Hensen was coyoting around the rim himself, but trying to get a flat-out commitment from Race. Race remembered what Jackson hinted about Hensen being behind his own troubles . . . unless the rancher just didn't measure Race up to be a full sixteen hands and was testing him. Just what the hell was Hensen getting at? Until the man cut the deck a little deeper, Race decided to give him an equally ambiguous answer.

"Well, Mr. Hensen, depends exactly which old line of work you're talking about. My back's pretty much against the wall. I still haven't sold my saddle, but it might come to that yet."

There, he thought to himself, let the old man chew on that—he can take it literal or local.

Hensen, like any cowman, knew a saddle was the single most important item in a cowboy's outfit. Without it, he might as well look to swamping out saloons for a living. But "sold his saddle" was also a cowboy—or local—expression with shadier connotations. A man who'd sell his saddle would do just about anything for a dollar.

Race's double entendre wasn't lost on Hensen and the rancher's eyes flickered in appreciation. The saddle tramp was a damn sight quicker than he'd first credited.

He asked Race, "Ride that trail one more time?"

Race shrugged. "That trouble I'd been in had nothing to do with the spread I worked for. What I'm saying is if I hire on, I ride for the brand, do what I'm told and mind my own business. You want anything more definite than that from me, you're going to have to spread your own hand clearer."

"Okay. By rights this outfit is mine, solo. I'd like to keep it that way. It'd be worth seventy-five a month to the right man to help me do just that. Seventy-five beats just bed and board."

Hensen laid it out pretty open and Race caught his drift. Anything that offered regular chuck and a bed out of the weather sorely tempted. Twice now he'd slaved and scrimped only to have the whole damn thing blow up in his face. And here Hensen was offering him gun wages.

Why the hell shouldn't he take it? Why not drift with the tide—you couldn't get lower than the bottom and that's where he was now. Of course, from what Jackson told him, it'd mean trouble for the women. Race wasn't sure just how far he could travel in that direction. And there was one more thing—the time he'd already done in the pen.

Reluctantly Race shook his head. "Your offer sure enough tempts hell out of me, Hensen, but I'd hate like hell to put in another seven years plaiting hoss-hair bridles up at Laramie."

Hensen got up to leave.

"About the other, what do you say?" Race tried one more time. "Will you let me hang on a few days?"

Wordlessly Hensen shook his head. Not now for sure. The drifter could too easy let something of this conversation slip. Taking up the bull's-eye lantern, the rancher plodded out of the barn.

Cursing in bitter frustration, Race wheeled suddenly and slammed his hand against the end stall. That was as close as he'd ever come to begging. And for what!

The taste of brass was in his mouth as he cut the lamp and groped his way to the loft in the darkness.

IX

The women leafed through a year-old almanac while the tea steeped on the cookstove.

"Here's one I missed before." Sage giggled, pointing to an advertisement for a "nose-straightening machine."

"Let me see." Libby leaned over her shoulder to look and laughed. "That's as bad as the 'bustle booster' I found last time." The two had a running contest to see who could find the most preposterous advertisements. "Ah, now here's something I need."

Sage looked quickly at Libby.

"I'm serious. With winter coming on in dead earnest, we should have a croop lamp."

"If you say so," Sage agreed. But mention of the croop lamp reminded her of something else. "Libby, are you sure those are cold sores on that drifter's mouth?"

"Sure . . . or fever blisters. Same thing. Why? What did you think they were?"

Sage flushed scarlet. "I was just wondering, that's all."

Libby looked at her closely. "The devil you were. Now tell me."

"Nothing. I just thought, well, those sores and all, you know."

"No, I don't know."

"You do, too. You just want to hear me say it. You've heard the very same stories about cowboys that I have."

"Sage! You didn't think . . . " Libby broke into laughter.

"Well, I'd heard stories," Sage defended sheepishly.

"Now that we're on the subject—of the drifter, that is—what was going on between you two at the table tonight?"

This time it was anger that reddened Sage's cheeks. "That cowboy has to be the crudest, most ignorant man I've ever had the displeasure of meeting."

"Probably the hungriest, too."

"What makes you say that, Lib?"

"At first I thought his mouth was too sore for him to chew his food. But after I watched him a bit, I realized he was having trouble keeping his food down."

"Oh, he was just fooling with his food. He wasn't even hungry."

"No. You're wrong. If he could have eaten, he'd have cleaned up that whole table. His stomach's just too badly shrunk to take in much food at a time. I really felt sorry for him. Lord knows the last time he put a meal under his belt."

"Libby, are you certain?" Sage's voice sounded far away even in her own ears.

Libby nodded. "Working with your parents, I saw enough half-starved Indians on the reservation to know. I'm sure."

Something heavy flipped over inside Sage and lay there like a burning lump.

". . . for I was an hungred, and ye gave me meat . . . ." Sage dropped her head into her hands. "And I claim to be a Christian."

"Sage, whatever are you talking about?"

"Cousin, I'm ashamed to tell you." But she did and when she finished, Libby nodded her head.

"What he needs is to eat regularly, a little bit at a time until he can handle normal amounts of food again. Don't feel bad, Sage." She patted the younger girl on the shoulder "You didn't know. Besides, drifters like him don't expect any better treatment, not really. Others must have done the same thing to him, otherwise he wouldn't be in such a bad way now."

Libby's attempt to console her only made Sage feel worse.

"I'd better take some food down to him."

"Do you think you should, Sage? Wouldn't it be better for us to fix something and let one of the men take it to him?"

Sage shook her head. "The men are all busy. Besides . . ." It was something Sage couldn't explain, because she didn't understand herself. But Libby understood.

"We'll fix something up and I'll go down with you."

"Thanks, Lib."

While the kettle of stew heated on the stove, Sage went upstairs to get her outdoor shoes. With a good-humored shake of her head, Libby moved closer to the stove and stirred in the dumplings. She'd never seen any man draw sparks out of Sage before. Maybe he had the steel to match her flint. It made Libby think of herself and of other, happier times.

Lost in memories of her own, Libby reminisced, unaware of anyone until an arm encircled her waist. Pivoting in surprise, she came full around into Maize Jackson's arms. With a start she pushed against his chest with her forearm, taking a backward step that landed her in the bunkroom doorway.

Added to his good looks, Maize had just enough mystery about him to stir a woman. But whatever attraction the gunman might offer was more than offset by a nameless fear Libby had of him. There was no sound reason for it, but it started when they had found Sage's parents and had grown ever since.

"What do you want, Maize?" Libby's voice was flat, not betraying any of the ambivalence she felt at his touch.

"I want you."

"I'm a married woman . . . did you forget?"

"Huh-uh, but I'm sure trying. Tell me, Lib, how long as it been since you had a man? Don't you miss it?"

Her mouth tight with anger, Libby tried to brush past Jackson to get back into the kitchen. But he raised an arm across the doorway, blocking her.

"Don't get mad at me. I'm just repeating what's common bunkhouse gossip. Bull ought to change his name to *Steer*."

"Look, Maize, I had my choice of marrying you or Bull. I made that choice. Maybe it was the right one and maybe it wasn't. But under any circumstances, it's none of your business. Now step aside and let me through."

"Oh, I can wait—for a while. But remember, patience isn't my long suit." As he talked, Jackson's hand moved lightly down Libby's cheek, down across her neck. Before his hand reached its obvious destination, Libby slapped it away. At that moment, Sage returned to the kitchen.

Wordlessly, Maize stepped aside to let Libby pass, his lips pulled back into a humorless grin.

Libby didn't look at Maize as she swept past him, but her voice trembled when she spoke. "You get the lantern, Sage, and I'll carry the kettle. Everything's ready."

Jackson stared after the women, wrapped up and going out the door with the kettle of stew. Only one place they could be heading. Maize rubbed his jaw.

Now wouldn't Bull be interested in finding his wife down to the barn with that drifter . . .

The narrow smile on his lips froze. Just inside the bunkroom door sat Jésus. The damned greaser heard everything he'd said to Libby.

Swearing under his breath, Jackson pushed the door shut with his bootheel.

"Old man," he said, "looks like you and me's gotta make a little *habla*."

The conversation was brief, to the point, and all one-sided. Jésus sat motionless throughout, his eyes glaring without fear at the gunman.

When Jackson finished, Jésus fingered away the tiny drops of blood from his bony chest where Maize had traced a cross with is Bowie.

"Señor Jackson," the old man hissed, "you made your mark on me with your knife. Now I swear to you before all the saints and before the devil himself, that one day my knife will return the favor. Ah, you look at this shrunken old body and smile. But I tell you, *chulo*, you are

55

muerto . . . dead."

"Swallow your threats, old man, before you swallow some lead." Jackson dismissed the *viejo's* threat, but a vague foreboding lingered.

Not long afterward, at the deal table, Jackson leaned over Bull Walker's shoulder and whispered into his ear.

X

The day's events and uncertainties left Race drained. Up in the loft he fixed himself a bed in the farthest corner of the outer wall and collapsed on it. Fine snow sifted through the cracks between the weathered boards. A cold location, but one providing relief from the rank ammonia smells of the stalls below.

Making a cocoon of his ravaged blanket, he burrowed deep under the loose hay. He shifted restlessly, strung too fine for sleep. The old shame and frustration lay bitterly on his mind.

Appetite wasn't on him, either, but he knew as a point of survival he'd have to force himself. As he gnawed indifferently on the pilfered chunk of beef, the vision he'd had that afternoon of him and Will scrounging food came back, taunting him. Most times he could clamp down unwanted thoughts before they got out of hand. But tonight they just triggered off a whole chain of moody reminiscing.

Like Libby and Bull Walker, Race's parents had been a total mismatch—his mother, a decent woman of solid Virginia-Texas stock; his father, a dour German immigrant who couldn't even laugh in good English. The latter proved no handicap, however, since the old man lacked any sense of humor.

It took a few years for them to reproduce and when a child finally did come, it came damaged. That was Will.

57

From that point on, the old man set out to prove he could produce upgrade offspring. As his private receiving chamber, his wife took on all the characteristics of a broodmare, dropping foals with disgusting regularity.

Race, the second of a whole string of kids to come, somehow became the scapegoat. Because the old man could never expect any returns from Will, he demanded twice as much from Race.

First job the old man ever lined up for him was swabbing dishes, pans, and floors at a local boarding house. Race wasn't sure how old he was at the time, but he remembered having to stand on a box to reach the dry-sink.

Schooling was out of the question. Because the old man couldn't read or write, he didn't see any need for the kids to. More important for them to work and bring home their earnings to him.

The one time Race talked his mother into countermanding this order resulted in near disaster. When they thought the old man was asleep, she had pulled out the Bible—her only book and last remaining tie with a family that had been wiped out years ago—and set in to teach Race to read. They had no more than got the Book out when the old man caught them. Beat hell out of Race and his mother both, then threw the Bible into the fire.

Not long after, while bearing her tenth child in less than that many years, Race's mother died. When she did, the old man took the money he'd been hoarding and disappeared, stranding the whole damn brood of kids. That was before Race's ninth birthday.

The time and place were postwar Texas. Hard times for all but the carpetbaggers. Still, the younger kids fared pretty well, different families taking them in. Race had his chance, too, but no one wanted to be saddled with Will. Hell, he couldn't blame them for that. On the other hand, he couldn't bring himself to desert the mentally and physically deficient older brother either. So Race took it on himself to support both of them.

Garbage heaps and dumping grounds provided their subsistence—food, clothing, rummagable items to trade or sell—but not enough to sustain Will. God, but it hurt like hell to watch him go downhill.

In desperation, Race had broken into a store, and taken what they needed. He discovered stolen food not only tasted better than the garbage they'd been eating, but it was a damn sight easier to come by. The discovery came too late to help his brother. Will never made it through that first winter.

After that Race played a lone hand except for the year he teamed up with "Ruby" Evans, a flashy Negro gambler who sported red glass cuff-links and stickpin. When their trails crossed, Ruby discovered that Race, with his quick reactions and the hard driving power of his long legs, could beat out most horses at distances under a hundred yards.

The two cleaned up around the cowtowns until they hit a place recently settled by Virginians and Carolinians. These newcomers had brought their short-coupled quartermilers West with them. Damn good horses, Race had to admit. Matter of fact, his own buckskin was one of the breed, only a little more refined than those early ones.

As it turned out, Race hadn't been a match for those horses and the partnership between man and boy got wiped out along with their stakes.

But in the year they had trailed together, Ruby had schooled him in the fundamentals of his particular calling. Ruby, a straight gambler, nevertheless knew all the tricks of the trade and taught them to Race so the boy could spot a sharper when he ran across one.

"Another thing you got to know if you take up gambling," Ruby told him, "is how to take care of yourself in a scrape. For myself, I prefer knives and razors, 'cause most of your fights is gonna be close-in anyway." His white teeth flashed as he said it. Well, he taught Race and Race was a good student.

Before they split up, Ruby did one more thing for him. Instead of leaving him on his own hook, the way he had found him, Ruby traveled several days out of his way to take Race to a cattle outfit in West Texas that a friend was rodding. Far as Race could recall, that was the one and

59

only time anyone had ever taken a foot out of the way to do him a good turn. The memory still warmed him.

Race's reminiscing carried him on to the ranch work, the cattle drives, to thoughts of Jen. But somehow the picture of her he tried to conjure failed, and he kept seeing Sage up there at the big house, the firelight playing warmly across her features.

You been too long without a woman, he told himself.

Head resting on interlaced fingers, the cowboy stared into the cold black emptiness of the barn, an unutterable sense of loneliness claiming him.

At what point he drifted off, or if he actually ever did, Race wasn't sure. But the instant one of the doors below swung open, he sprang alert and edged quietly to the loft overhang.

Sage appeared in the small circle of light thrown off by the lamp she carried. He wondered what brought her down to the barn alone. Hard on that thought, sudden heat shot up along the insides of his thighs.

Cut out that thinking, damn you. She's a woman, sure enough—but not that kind.

With effort, Race redirected his thoughts. And when he spoke, none of the agitation Sage's unexpected visit stirred up showed in his slow even drawl.

"Can I help you with something, ma'am?"

She took a few steps closer, trying to see beyond the lantern glare.

"May I see you a minute?"

"You bet."

Rather than fumblefoot down the ladder, Race gripped the edge of the loft and lightly swung down. As he limped toward her, he brushed the hay from his clothes. A half-formed smile froze on his lips as he caught her staring at his off-rhythm gait. Self-conscious he drew up stiff, made a deliberate effort to even up his stride and stopped an arm's length away from her.

He'd mentioned being broken up by a horse. And she'd

noted peculiarities in his walk, attributing them to saddle-stiffness, the snow, the icy steps. But she'd never put the two ideas together. Only now did full realization come . . . and she understood the reason his leg butted up against hers at the supper table.

Race shifted uncomfortably. Without looking up at him, Sage held out the kettle. "I brought this down for you."

As he took the kettle from her, the lid tilted. Race's stomach jerked tight as the rich aroma steamed up at him.

He looked at her, unable to keep the broad smile from his face. "Why this's real good of you, Miss Hensen."

Sage vaguely resented that he should appear so relaxed while she . . . well, what was she?

"Don't misunderstand. It's just some stew and I'd have done it for anybody."

"That's beside the point. Far as I'm concerned, it's turkey dinner with all the trimmings. It's funny your doing this. What I mean is, I was just laying back thinking of somebody else who'd done me a real nice turn, too—by name of Ruby Evans."

"Kin of yours?"

"Lord, no!" A grin worked across Race's face as he wondered what the flamboyant black man would think of that! "Ruby's just a real good friend picked me up at a hell—" Race started to say hell-hole, caught and corrected himself, "—at a place I was working as a kid. I was close on to the brink of manhood and Ruby kind of gave me a nudge in the right direction."

"Indeed!" Sage's cheeks flamed. She'd caught Race's slip of the tongue and the rest wasn't hard to figure, nor the kind of nudge that Ruby woman had probably given him. That this drifter should be so crude as to compare her with some saloon tart!

"Well, I've wasted enough time here. See that you clean the pot before you return it in the morning."

"Why sure, ma'am." Race eyed her doubtfully having picked up the sudden change in her manner. But as hungry for company as food tonight, Race ventured, "It's still storming. I'll walk you back to the hou—''

''You will not.'' Sage broke in sharply. She knew she was overreacting, but she didn't know why. Anything the cowboy did was his business, yet she couldn't curb her unreasonable disgust with the man.

In an attempt to take her rebuff in stride, he said. ''Well, I'm still obliged for the food. Maybe tomorrow before I pack on out you'll have some chores lined up for me to handle to pay you back.''

''I didn't think range bums ever bothered to pay anything back.''

A long drawn-out silence followed. At last Race said, ''I know I got off on the wrong foot with you today and I'm not blaming anyone for that but myself. It's pretty obvious I just said or did something else to set you off again. That I honest to God don't know what it was speaks even more poor of me, I guess. But I do want you to know, whatever it was, it wasn't done intentional. I just have to beg humble against a cowpuncher's ignorance.''

His reply was out of keeping with the image she had built of him in her mind of an insensitive grub-line riding parasite. She searched his face for a hidden irony or sarcasm, but found neither.

She opened her mouth to speak, but whatever she proposed to say was drowned in a clap and stir behind her. Libby's body careened across the dirty floor—Race's first intimation that Sage hadn't come down alone after all. His eyes followed the blur that was Libby.

''My God, what—'' then he caught another movement off to the left. Bull Walker, standing just inside the door thumbed back the hammer of his .45 as he raised it.

With a sweep of his right arm, Race shoved Sage clear, and with is left heaved the cast-iron kettle. It caught Bull square under the short ribs. Walker's look had followed his first moved, causing him to pause in brief confusion as his mind registered Sage's presence.

The solid impact of the iron pot knocked Walker off his pins, sent the gun skittering. Race went after the gun instead of after Walker. He had no desire to plunge into a wrestling match with a man nearly double his bulk.

The two men collided as they dove for the gun. As they hit the ground, Race jerked his elbow back and up several times in rapid succession, catching Walker in the throat on each backswing, groping for the gun on the forward swing. He got his fingertips on it and dragged it in, toward his body. Walker rolled to the side, gathered himself and sprang, landing flat on Race's back.

Air whooshed out of Race's lungs, his face ground into the hard-packed earth. The gun was under his body, digging him in the chest as Bull's straddling weight pinned him over it.

Bull's ham-like fists pounded against Race's sore ribs. Race brought his elbow back again, drove it sharply against the point of Walker's hip. The heavier man contracted involuntarily, giving Race the wedge he needed.

Gasping in air, Race bunched his muscles and straightened suddenly. He caught the 3-H segundo by surprise and threw him off. Walker scrambled around on the ground, trying to get back on top of Race, but the cowboy's gunhand was free now and he rolled in the opposite direction, grabbed the gun and slammed it into Bull's face. The gunsight ripped Walker across the temple, down the length of his face. The blow halted Walker only momentarily, then he was coming on again.

Race vaulted to his feet, trying to keep out of Walker's reach, but one of Bull's meaty hands fastened around Race's ankle and jerked him heavily to the ground. Race's spine felt as if it had shattered under him. Writhing in pain, he saw Bull collect himself into a crouch and leap. Once Walker was airborne, Race folded back his good leg, knee to chest and kicked out. The heel of his boot landed under Walker's chin, just above the Adam's apple.

The segundo's head snapped back violently and he dropped to the floor like a poleaxed steer. Race picked up the gun and, cocking it, pulled himself up against the stall, watching Walker for any further signs of fight.

Leaning against the beam, Race drew in painfully ragged breaths. He had to empty his mouth of barn dirt and blood before asking Sage, "You all right?"

She nodded.

"Miz Walker?"

"I guess so. At least she's awake now. That ape knocked her out!"

Race nodded, gulping for air. "But why, for God's sake? What the hell got into that son-of-a—" Race broke off, remembering to keep the lid on his can of cuss-words.

"He doesn't need a reason." She paused. "He must have seen Libby coming down here and thought she was alone with you."

Race did swear then. "Goddamn any man that would hit a woman!" Race wished Bull would wake up so he could lay him out again.

Libby pushed herself up to a sitting position, head resting heavily in her hands.

"I'll be all right. He's never done anything like this before." She tried to get up. "I'd better stop that bleeding on his head. Might be a cut artery."

Race wanted to shout at her to *let the bastard bleed*. But he held his tongue and helped Libby get Bull to his feet. With her slim shoulder under her husband's, Libby led Bull out of the barn.

Sage and Race stood together, watching. When the other two got outside, Race let the gun off cock. Sage asked him about it, but he shook his head.

"I'll keep this for now," he said.

Sage arched her eyebrows but offered no comment. When she got outside, she locked the barn doors.

"Thanks, lady," Race murmured through swollen lips.

Stiffly he stepped to the overturned kettle to see what he could salvage. What hadn't spilled over Walker had been sucked up by the thirsty dirt floor.

"Dammit. *Dammit to hell!*"

XI

Next time Race Evans' body hit the hay pallet, he fell dead asleep. He figured nothing else could happen tonight and if it did, he didn't give a damn. All he wanted was some sleep.

But he'd underestimated his system's sharply honed instinct for survival. At first, he tried to ignore the smell. He buried his head against it. He fought it. But the nose-pinching smell of kerosene persisted, penetrating the level just below consciousness. Then came the crackling sound and Race woke instantaneously all senses alert, his first thought was to free the animals. Less than ten seconds elapsed between the time he first scented the coal-oil and the time his mind registered *fire*!

For the second time that evening he swung down from the loft, this time speeding directly to the doors. He tried them, only then remembering Sage had locked them from the outside.

He lost precious time clambering up the ladder back onto the loft. Smoke was already filtering through on that side when he remembered the small door off the front of the loft. He groped for the opening, driving splinters into his fingers. Tracing the outline of the loft door with his hand, he found and turned the block fastener and pushed. The door skreaked on rusty hinges but gave easily enough. Like most barns, this had a protruding beam from which pulley and tackle were mounted for lifting hay.

Working hand over hand to the end of the beam, Race caught hold of the gant line and slid to the ground. His bad leg barely hampered him as he raced to the doors, and threw them open. Back inside he caught the buckskin's halter and led her out, the others nervously following. He locked the doors again to prevent any of the animals from returning to the barn while he ran to the house for help.

As Race cornered the barn, he caught a glimpse of a brief flare of light, a small figure's outline, then a blinding burst of flame as the whole side of the barn ignited. The first explosive thrust of the kerosene-fed fire licked at Race, spotlighting and singeing him at the same time. Race leaped back from the searing heat just as a slug clipped past his head.

The comforting weight of Walker's .45 lay between his waist and belt band. Race jerked it out and snapped off a shot. Missed. On the second shot, the small man spun, regained his balanced and helled out of there. From the way the man jumped, Race was sure he scored a hit. He started after him, but stopped, deciding that saving the barn was more important.

Using his bare hands, Race started shoveling snow onto the flames. Before long the crew, tumbled out of their sacks and half-dressed, were alongside him, helping.

It lacked an hour to dawn when Race had first discovered the fire. By first light, the last ember was killed. The fire didn't take hold against the snow-dampened wood as it ordinarily would in that dry climate.

Examination of the damage showed it to be considerably less than they first feared. The firewood stacked at the back corner of the barn was destroyed, but the building itself suffered little real damage. The few badly charred boards could easily be replaced. Miraculously, the hay was untouched.

The hands mulled around in weary silence while Libby and Sage poured coffee. Race accepted his, and dropped exhausted onto a log. Bandy dropped beside him. Too tired for talk, they just sat, sipping their hot drinks.

Suddenly the silence took on a different timbre. Lifting

his head against the acute stillness, Race discovered the crew casually ringing him. Bandy slid off the log, and stepped away from Race.

Eyes roving from one face to another, Race set his cup to the ground and rose slowly. A quick glimpse placed the barn just two steps to his rear.

Hensen asked, "You got those matches I gave you last night?"

Race patted his pockets, shook his head.

"That you doing the shooting?"

"Some of it."

"Thought you didn't have no gun."

In a deliberately slow move—so his action wouldn't be misunderstood—Race withdrew the Colt. "Picked this off the floor of the barn last night."

Race chose his words carefully, not knowing what, if anything, passed after his set-to with Walker last night.

"Uh-huh. Lost your matches and found a gun."

"That's right." Race backed up, and lazily leaned against the barn. There was no threat in the move, but it was understood by every man there he had just put himself in a better position in case he needed it.

Walker said, "Looks like my gun. Must have dropped it up in the loft last night when Maize and me went up to get him." He aimed a thumb a Race.

Hensen noticed the clotted gash across Bull's temple. He looked from one man to the other.

Bull said, "I'll take it back now, Evans."

Race shook his head. "Later." Walker didn't argue the point and no one else did either.

"Uh-huh," Hensen said again. Then, "How'd the fire start?"

"Smelled like coal-oil to me. It was set deliberate."

"I've already figgered that out. But outside of the crew—all of which was bedded down up to the house—that leaves only you, Evans."

"And the man I shot at. I think I might've barked him."

"That so? Get a good look at him?"

" 'Bout all I could tell, he was small built." For the first

67

time, Race hedged around the truth. In that flash of light, Race had clearly seen Kell Farley.

When Sage had thrown that name at him yesterday, it had jumped his nerves. Last he knew, Farley was still at Nebraska—supposedly for life. But just let Race try to explain any of that to this snakebit crew.

Sage stood just behind Hensen, holding Race in steady regard. From her look Race knew that she knew he was lying. There was an unconscious plea in his eyes. Race relaxed as Sage turned and walked back to the house.

He looked back to Hensen, who was kneading his forehead with his knuckles. "Keno," Hensen said, "you and Lin take a look. See if you can cut sign of anybody else." Hensen swore half to himself, "That damn Paiute's never around when you need him."

They waited in tense silence for the cowboys to report back. What they offered when they did was skimpy.

"Well, hell, boss," Keno said, "we ain't no damn trackers. The loose hosses scattered . . . messed up everything . . . well, hell, we ain't trackers."

Shaking his head in disgust, Hensen again confronted Race. "Strikes me damn funny my barn gets fired same night I turn you down for a job of work. On the other hand, some bronc trying to make himself look good with the boss might rig a deal like this. You wouldn't care to change your story any, would you, Evans?"

"Not any." Sparks had scorched new holes in his already ragged clothes. The stench of singed hair on his hands and face rose to feed the fire building inside him. He knew what Hensen was getting at. That conversation they had had last night wasn't one the big augur would want repeated and he'd run Race off on a rail given the slightest justification. Likely he'd prefer something even more permanent if he could force an issue.

Eyes vibrant with controlled anger, Race strung his words out, the Texas drawl unconsciously broadening.

"We both know what you're getting at, Hensen. I've handed you the straight goods and you know that too. Now you can take 'er up or leave 'er off. The choice is yours."

The rancher grunted knowing he was hanging both sides over a barrel. "You got ten minutes to get your self the hell out of here. And give Walker his gun back . . . *now*."

That forced a smile to Race's lips and he shook his head. "I'll leave it up to the house when I pull out." He waited until the yard cleared before he stepped away from the barn.

Just as he set the rigging on his mare, the Paiute came helling into the ranchyard. Some words were exchanged and at a shout from Hensen, all hands made to their mounts. Within minutes the crew followed out after the Indian.

More trouble for Hensen, Race guessed. He led the dressed buckskin up to the house and rapped on the door. Libby answered. Race touched fingertips to hatbrim.

"Just returning the kettle and your husband's gun. How are you this morning? Didn't get a chance to ask before."

"Oh, fine," she said, but kept the left side of her face averted. "Come in and have some breakfast."

"I'd appreciate something, but I'd better not come in. Hensen give me ten minutes to drag my freight and time's just about up."

"Can't see that a few minutes either way would make that much of a difference."

A sardonic smile lifted the corners of his mouth.

"I'm inclined to agree with you, ma'am, but I doubt Hensen or your husband would see it that way."

Libby returned his smile. "I can't argue that. Wait just a minute then, and I'll have Jésus throw some trail rations together for you."

When Libby returned with the grubsack, Race peered over her shoulder, hoping to catch a glimpse of Sage. With a little twinge of disappointment, he took the sack from Libby.

"Obliged. Would you thank Miss Hensen for me . . . I think she'll know what for."

Just then Libby turned her head and Race saw the purple blotch. He swore bitterly to himself.

Seeing the change in his expression, Libby stepped back, covering her face.

69

Race stared at her. "I only wish . . ." but whatever it was he wished, he left unsaid. Tipping his hat, he wheeled away knowing better than to get further involved with any more 3-H problems. He couldn't even handle his own.

As he took up the reins, Race looked at the sky. Snow clouds hung low and heavy.

He gigged the buckskin south.

XII

As he examined his arm where Race's chance shot pinked him, Farley did more damning than a saw-dust preacher. The other men in the one-room shack mulled around in uncomfortable silence, not wanting to draw his ravings to themselves.

"That son-of-a-bitch Jackson set me up. I know he did!"

"Mebbe one of the hands was just out for a midnight stroll to the sandbox," Stubbs volunteered.

"Nah. Wasn't one of Hensen's hands—not no regular, anyhow. I knowed this dirty son and he knowed me. Couldn't of been no one but Jackson sicced him on me."

"Who is he?"

"Can't rec'lect his name right off, but him and me done some time together a few years back."

Stubbs threw down his quirly and ground it out on the floor. "So now just where the hell does this leave the rest of us?"

"Huh! Damned if I know."

"But if that fancy sport is runnin' a whizzer on us . . ."

"That's what we got to find out. Keep your ears and eyes peeled back damn fine. We'll string that smart bastard along until he out-coyotes himself.

"Bern, you better come with me to Pipe Spring. I'm going to brace Jackson about this and if I need you, you

71

can back up my hand. Stubbs, orders are for you to raise some hell over to Hensen's while we got him and his crew tolled off. Just scare them petticoats—don't mess with 'em, not yet anyway. We don't want to do nothing to bring them Mormons down on our necks. Right now they don't give much of a damn what happens to Hensen—he's been about as neighborly as a cornered skunk.''

"How come I'm to handle it alone?''

"I handled last night alone, didn't I?''

"Yeah, and you got shot.''

"Won't nobody be there but two skirts and that old Mex.''

"What about your bunky from lonesome stony?''

"If he's workin' for Hensen, he'll be with him. Just keep your eyes open so if he is there, you see him first. Paiute, you collect Hensen and his crew and herd them toward Pipe Spring. Tell him looks like someone besides me run his cattle this time. Let him worry.

"Shesty, you and Jason work them 3-H cattle east of Squaw Spring. Head them toward the bunch Stevens's holding this side of Sourdough Well. We're getting a pretty good bunch gathered. Once Jackson gives the word, we'll take .'em all.''

It didn't take Race long to discover the route he'd chosen wasn't a particularly good one. The ground kept rising, tiring the mare early. The trees grew thicker and whatever small trail he was following seemed to lead to nowhwere.

Compared to yesterday, his situation hadn't changed appreciably. If anything, it was worse. He was afoot, leading his horse. Each step reminded him of the burns and assorted bruises he'd accumulated since yesterday. The game leg throbbed with pain the length of it and his limp, more pronounced because of it, slowed his progress.

As he traveled, he saw nothing resembling a working ranch or even a trapper's digs. Ugly clouds darkened the sky and as the winds picked up, the air became even colder.

Two hours shy of noon, Race broke through the dense evergreen canopy onto a ragged jumble of rocks. Passing between two enormous boulders that stood like two old maids at a keyhole, he found himself at the brink of . . . nothing. A thousand feet below a rolling everchanging cloud cover played around mesa tops and temple peaks that, like icebergs, showed only a portion of what lay below.

He couldn't help wonder at its beauty in spite of the predicament it put him in. Grand Canyon just didn't say it.

A spooky kind of chill shuddered through Race. "Let's get the hell away from here, hoss."

He backed the buckskin through the cut away from the rim, then unlooped the grubsack from the saddlehorn. As he munched on a dry biscuit, he tried to figure out his next step.

So far as he could tell, no break existed along the rugged rim where a man could take a horse. That ungodly hole in the ground wrapped around as far as the eye could see, blocking passage anyway but northwest—the direction he had just come from. Then there was this new snowstorm dogging him.

His only alternative, as he saw it, was to backtrack all the way to Hensen's. But that wouldn't be easy. It meant heading directly into the face of the oncoming storm.

His reception if and and when he got there was another prospect he didn't relish.

Race cursed the stubborn pride that had kept him from asking anyone at the ranch which way to head out. But pride was all he was operating on lately and he came damn close enough to losing even that these past twenty-four hours.

Reluctantly he set off, knowing each minute's delay put him and the mare in further jeopardy. Like yesterday's squall, the storm came on him suddenly. Only this wasn't some shotgun snow squall blowing in and out in one explosive blast. This was a dyed-in-the-wool blue norther, nature run wild and bound and determined to bury everything in sight under frigid layers of ice and snow.

In nothing flat the temperatures dropped to zero and the bitter winds drove them deeper. Ice crusted over yesterday's snow, its sharp edges cutting the mare's fetlocks each time she broke through. Race had to stop each time to pull shards of ice from her coronets.

He didn't even attempt to ride her, as much to keep his own body going and to keep in touch with reality, as to spare the animal. The wind's relentless roar tortured his ears, scoured his face raw even though he walked as much leeward of the mare as possible. His movements became automatic, numbness consuming his hands and feet, then his arms and legs. He had to look at his feet to reassure himself he was still moving.

The numbness was a real danger Race recognized, yet he blessed the relief it gave him from the constant ragged pain that had been shooting up and down his left leg.

Landmarks he'd troubled to memorize earlier were useless now, the whirling eddies of snow creating a white void. At first, he set his course by the wind. But as he became more exhausted and disoriented, he had to rely on the buckskin's instincts and hoped to God she was heading for the ranch.

Once, he stumbled, falling away from the mare. It took him anxious minutes to relocate the animal as she moved away from him. If he got separted from her again, he knew it'd be good-bye, that's all she wrote for him.

He wrapped the reins around his wrist. If he fell again, he might get dragged or he might even lose a hand to the gangrene, but if the buckskin made it to shelter, he'd be there with her. His thinking became confused as the storm pounded him to near insensibility, but he pushed doggedly on.

What seemed hours later, the buckskin hesitated, pricked her ears forward, then picked up her gait, nearly dragging Race along. Then it came to him, teasing him back into a state of semi-alertness. There it was again—the smell of woodsmoke.

The words shot from him—

"By God, we're home!"

XIII

"Aw, this's been nothing but a damn wild-goose chase. What the hell am I paying you for anyway?" Hensen railed at his Paiute tracker, getting a noncommittal shrug in reply.

"Wait here," he told the others. "With this damn storm, looks like we're gonna have to lay over. I'll see if they can put us up overnight."

Hensen entered the redstone fort at Pipe Spring and spoke to Pulsipher, the Mormon currently in charge. Sleeping arrangements settled, the superintendent quartered Hensen's crew in one of the barracks-like dugouts outside the fort's walls, three to a room. He provided Hensen, however, with one of the small comfortable rooms on the second floor within the enclosed main building.

Although the hour was late, Pulsipher rounded up grub for Hensen and his outfit. In answer to Hensen's inquiries concerning his driven stock, no one had seen or heard anything—or so they claimed.

To himself, Hensen granted that could be true. In this storm a dozen head could have been pushed unnoticed within yards of the fort.

Dissatisfaction and worry rode Hensen hard as he made his way back to his room. Losses to the rustlers would be small potatoes compared to what a sustained storm might hack out of his herds.

It was typical of Hensen that he'd be worrying about his cattle rather than the women back at his ranch.

Hell, he told himself, my half-sister got along for twenty-two years before leeching onto me, and that other one ain't even kin. He resented them and the high-handed way they came in and tried to take over. Hell with 'em both.

Hensen held a match to a flat-wicked lamp near the door. Dull light glowed through its smoke-grimed chimney. Rattling through his saddlebags, he scared up the flask he'd bundled there. Shucking his outer coat, Hensen eased onto the sagging rope bed with a long sigh. He pulled on the flask, sighed again as the biting warmth of the whiskey stole through him.

As he drained a second slug of the liquor, a voice from the shadow near the wood-stove cut across the room.

"Ain't you gonna share that with a friend?"

Hensen almost choked on his drink as the little outlaw Kell Farley stepped into the dim circle of light.

"By damn! What are you doing here! You got a helluva nerve sneaking into my room!"

"Yeah, I got that all right. Got something else, too. Got another business proposition for you."

Hensen grunted. "What do you want to do? Sell me my cattle back?"

Farley laughed. "Look, those nickel and dime raids haven't been hurting you any and they're barely enough to keep me and the boys in drinking money. Besides, you agreed to lay off me and my crew if we'd throw a scare into those petticoats."

"For all the good that's done so far. They're still there, aint they?"

Farley shrugged. "That's the proposition I got to make you. Worked right, it could make you'n me both happy. Wanna hear it?"

"Don't cost nothing to listen."

"For a quarter of your herd, I'll—"

"A quarter of my herd!" Hensen nearly jumped off the bed.

"Why not? Way it is now, you got to fork over two-thirds of every damn thing you got—including buildings and land—to them two women. A quarter of your herd ain't much for me and my boys for just this one time. Once I cash in, I'm cutting out. I don't crave to spend no more time in this frost-bit section of hell than I have to."

"Yeah, well what do I get in exchange for my four hundred head of cattle?"

"I just told you. You get rid of them girls and me once and for all."

"What I meant was how. I don't want them around, but I don't want no female blood on my conscience, either."

"Nah, nothing like that. Hell, you think I want to sport a hemp necktie? Look. You keep your crew off our backs while we make the big gather. We'll snake 'em across the border into southern Utah. I got a buyer there who'll keep his mouth shut."

"So what does that buy me? You run off my beef, fat chance I'll have of seeing you again, let alone my money."

"You gotta trust somebody. If you sell your stuff off at Lund where you always do, word'll get back and Jackson'll see that them women get their cut. But if rustlers run off your herds, there won't be no money for you to fork over to them."

"So? The outfit is still worth plenty. They know that."

"That's where the rest of my plan comes in, Hensen. Now tell me honest—if someone was to hold your sister, what would you give to get her back?"

"Not a damn thing!"

"What I figgered, but who else knows that?"

"Nobody."

"There's your answer."

"Chew that a little finer, Farley. You lost me."

"All right. We take your sister and hold her a couple of days. You tell the Walker woman we got your sister and won't turn her back until you cough up ten thousand or whatever your place is worth. You tell her you gotta sell the whole outfit to get her back and it's gotta be kept on the Q.T. otherwise you'll get your sister back in little pieces in a burlap sack.

"Walker might balk, but his woman won't and her say-so is the one that counts. What I'm sayin' make sense to you?"

"On the face of it." Hensen rubbed his face. "If the girls figgered that between rustlers and ransom the outfit is busted, there'd be no reason for them to hang around no more."

"You got it. What d'you say? Do we deal?"

Farley's suggestion wasn't far off from what he'd had in the back of his mind when he approached Race Evans last night. And now with somebody else hitting his herds—at least that's what the Paiute told him—maybe he should take what he could out of the outfit while there was still something to take. Get ride of the women, sell out, move to Frisco, maybe buy into some kind of business.

Hensen knuckled his forehead. "Yeah, Farley, we deal. But we still got some fine points to work out. I'll get word to you through the Paiute. You can get in touch with me the same way. I'll tell him. Damn breed's too stupid to understand what's going on anyway.

"Just remember one thing—about my sister. That ransom's a bluff, pure and simple. I meant what I said—I wouldn't pay one damn red cent to get her back, and you hurt her, you're strictly on your own."

"I'll drink to that!" Farley snatched the flask from Hensen, took a few hard swallows and handed it back. "I'll be in touch."

"No you won't, dammit. Use the Paiute."

Neither man offered to shake hands and Farley slipped quietly out of Hensen's room.

A brief flutter of conscience made Hensen uneasy. But another long pull at the flask set it to rest.

XIV

The monotonous slog of horse and cowboy ended abruptly as they came against the log-pole daypen where the *caballada* bunched in one corner. Now that the mare found the other horses, she yielded only reluctantly to her master's tug on the reins, as he led her past the haystacks around the side of the barn.

As he approached the first of the double doors, Race almost blundered into a hail of lead. A rifle poked blindly from between the slit doors, its roar muffled by the greater clamor of the storm.

Reacting without thinking, Race snaked out his free hand, fastened onto the protruding barrel and yanked. The startled rifleman clung to his weapon and crashed out through the doors right behind it.

Race shook free the reins of his humping horse, groping through the confused mass for the man's holstered gun. He got his fingers on it and in one fluid motion lifted the gun and spun to face the attacker.

During that same flurry of action, Farley's man Stubbs hit the frozen ground, slid spinning on his knees, ending up facing Race, his rifle lined on the cowboy's middle.

His own wild yell ringing in his ears, Race dove frantically to the ground. A slug grooved the air where he'd been standing. Hurriedly, Stubbs fired off another round before Race could trigger off his first.

Stubbs' second bullet sliced across Race's shoulder, taking a solid chunk of hide with it. But Race—prone, braced on elbow points—took time to aim before stroking trigger.

Stubbs' head jerked violently, his hand rising reflexively to the bullet's impact. His body hurtled backwards, bounced once on the frozen ground and was still. Stubbs had bought it.

Still on the ground, Race let out his breath, and dropped his head on folded arms. He'd seen dead men before, but he'd really done a job on this one. The back of the shattered skull had a hole almost big enough for Race to stick his fist in.

Soon as he got himself collected, Race looked toward the house, wondering what in hell was going on. From here though, he couldn't even see the outline of the place and had no idea what the situation might be. If anyone had been in the barn behind him, they'd have taken chips by now. But the house—well, that was just one more problem to face.

Rising on his good knee, Race reached forward, grabbed Stubbs by the ankle and dragged him into the barn. His thoughts were still out of focus and what to do next didn't come easy. The bullet crease across his shoulder burned like hell. He checked it and decided he'd live, but his old brush jacket had had it.

Race peeled off the bushwhacker's sheepskin-lined shortcoat and traded off. "Turn-about is fair play," he mumbled, and dropped his own frazzled jacket over the dead man's face.

While he had no desire to get further embroiled in the affairs of this haywire outfit, by his lights, Race owed the women something. And so far as he knew, they were up at the house by themselves, with just old Jésus for whatever help he could give them. Besides, if he had any intention of weathering out the storm at Hensen's place, he'd damn well better find out just how the land did lie.

Gun in fist, Race worked a cautious circle around the house, keeping well away from the dog pen. Since he had to go it blind, no reason to let an excitable dog give somebody else an advantage.

If he remembered right, the back door leading into the parlor was solid wood without glass panels. Climbing onto the gallery at a blind corner, he snaked along, hugging the wall, ducking under windows, until he reached that back door.

Rising, he leaned back, cocked his good leg and let fly. The door rocketed open, Race following it right in, diving to the floor.

An explosion of shot whistled over his head, taking out one of the back windows. Automatically Race thumbed hammer and fired. Almost too late he realized the shot had come from Sage's scattergun. Even as he was triggering, the fact hit home, giving him that fraction of a second to pull his shot.

Whitefaced, he yelled, "Hold it!"

"You!" Sage's finger tightened on the second trigger, sending Race scrambling forward. His shoulder caught her across the thighs, sending her sprawling.

"Hold fire, dammit!" Race yelled again as he wrestled with her on the floor. "You're the damn shootin'est woman I ever locked horns with!"

"Don't you swear at me, you—you saddlebum!"

"Then don't you shoot at me!" Roughly he wrenched the scattergun away from Sage and dragged her to her feet. Hands clamping her shoulders, he shook her. "Dear God, do you realize how close I come to plugging you just now?" Just thinking about it rocked Race down to his bootheels.

"No closer than you've been coming all day."

"Now what the hell's that supposed to mean?"

She didn't answer, but slowly the gist of her statement sank in as he took time to look at the wreckage strewn about—broken glass, splintered wood, kerosene from the bullet-riddled overhead lamp dripped from the dinner table onto the floor.

"You don't think I . . . Lady, I know what a damn poor opinion you hold of me, but even you couldn't think I had a hand in this! Ah, hell! Where are Jésus and Miz Walker?"

"That's none of your business." Libby was upstairs in the bedroom and Jésus was in the bunkroom on the other side of the house, keeping watch from their respective niches. But Sage wasn't about to give the drifter that information.

"All right, then *you* tell me what's been going on."

"You know that better than I do."

"Damnation, woman!" Out of patience, Race dipped a shoulder and slung Sage over it. With her hanging like a sack over his shoulder, he climbed through the opening where the front window used to be, through the storm to the barn.

Hearing a different clangor above the roar of the storm, Libby wondered what the sniper's random hazing hit now. She started down the stairs to check on Sage and ask her about it.

As she rounded the base of the steps, she saw a sheepskin-coated figure, Sage draped across him, step over the windowsill out onto the porch.

Fear turning her legs to leaden stumps, Libby treadmilled to the bunkroom to get Jésus.

Race had him a few wild moments there, struggling to open the barn doors with one hand while hanging onto a kicking, punching Sage with the other.

Without ceremony he unloaded her, grabbed her wrist, and hauled her over to Stubbs' body.

"There's your damn gulcher!" As he said it, he toed his old jacket off Stubbs' face.

Sage shuddered violently as if she couldn't make up her mind to faint or to be sick. She'd probably never seen a dead man before let alone one with half his head torn away.

Race swore at himself for his stupidity in dragging her down here, but hell, she made him mad. Contrite, he shrugged out of his newly acquired coat and wrapped it around the girl's shoulders. As he started to lead her away, Libby and Jésus burst in.

"Race? What are you doing here? What's going on?" Libby held the long-barrelled Peacemaker in her hand.

Using few words, Race explained.

Then Libby lit into him, reading the Scriptures at him

82

like they'd never been read before. Race took the tongue-lashing quietly. He had no quarrel with Libby and he had been dead wrong in lugging Sage down here.

When Libby finished raking him over the coals, he aimed a thumb at Stubbs and asked, "Any of you recognize him?"

They didn't.

Shivering, Race bent over Stubbs, picked up his own bloodspattered canvas jacket and started to put it on.

Horror mingled with contempt as Sage demanded, "What kind of man are you? Stealing clothes off a dead man!"

Race blinked, trying to pull his scattered thoughts together. "You got your spurs tangled, ma'am. This is my jacket. That's the gulcher's coat you got on."

Green tinged Sage's pale face. With a sound that defied description, she tore off Stubbs' jacket and hit for the house like a prairie chicken with a coyote on its tail.

Anticipating another verbal lacing, Race sheepishly faced Libby. But a broad grin split her face. Race returned a guilty grin, lifting his hands in a gesture of helplessness.

"Look," he said, "you all go on back to the house with Miss Hensen. I'll take care of this . . . ." He nudged Stubbs' body with his boot toe.

Alone again in the barn, Race made a concentrated effort to cinch up his thoughts. First he looked at Stubbs' horse. It was already in the barn, but Race turned him into the daypen with the rest of Hensen's cavvy. While he was out there, he rounded up his own buckskin.

About to put her with the others, he decided against it. She deserved better. So he put her in one of the stalls—at least until Hensen returned.

After tending the mare's needs, he got to the more grisly chores. Race stripped Stubbs down to the skin, then rolled him in a piece of tarp.

Next, he sorted through the man's clothing and personal items. Wasn't much there and Race folded those pocket stuffings into the dead man's scarf.

In addition to the single action Colt Race had acquired

earlier, Stubbs carried a lever-action repeating Winchester that, like the pistol, took .44-40's.

Shucking his tattered boots, he tried Stubbs' on for size. A little large, but in reasonably good condition.

He set these beside the wadded bundle of clothing and the rifle and went outside. He found the ground too frozen to dig even a shallow grave. So he dragged the tarp-covered corpse out of the barn, behind the building where it'd at least be out of sight of the house.

"Hell of a send-off—even for a drygulcher," were the only words Race said over the dead man.

Exhausted as he was, Race wanted nothing so bad as to crawl into a corner and bed down clear around the clock. But they'd be needing help with that mess up at the house.

Wearily he trudged up there and went in without knocking. All three were in the large room sweeping up while the winds sliced through the broken windows. Race walked directly to Libby, handed her the filled neck scarf.

"That poke's got all the 'gulcher's belongin's in it. You might want to sort through, see if you can't find something to identify him. His spurs might be worth something and there's a couple gold eagles. They ought to go some toward covering the damage he done."

"They will. Thank you."

Jésus kept working, but Sage stood watching them. Avoiding her steady regard, Race said to Libby, "I'm keeping his guns and these here, barring objections." Color worked up his neck as he indicated the roll of clothing. He already had Stubbs' boots and shortcoat on. At Sage's disgusted snort, his color deepened further, but he kept his focus on Libby. He really needed these items and he hoped she'd understand.

"Ma'am?" he prompted.

Biting on her lower lip, she glimpsed at Sage, then said, "No objections so far as I'm concerned. Keep them."

Nodding his thanks, Race suggested, "I'll cover those windows for you if you got something for me to work with."

Jésus led Race to one of the little storerooms built under

the porch. Hensen had some extra glass panes stored there—not enough for all the windows, but Race could board up the rest.

The size and dank smells of the cell-like room dredged up memories that worked a sick chill through Race. Preferring the rigor of the storm, he stepped outside and let Jésus hand the materials out to him.

For the next hour and a half he worked, each minute like an hour as his movements became more sluggish. His thoughts refused to stay in focus, and chills washed over him in waves.

Finally finished, he bent to pick up the tools and scraps. A strange, draining numbness started at the top of his head, spreading downward. He lost control of his motion and fell heavily across the heaped pile, teetering on the fringe of awareness, but unable to move or speak.

Voices came to him and drifted away in indistinct tides. He felt someone stripping the sheepskin coat from him and he fought them. They let him keep it on, and he relaxed.

Then someone was forcing hot liquid between his lips—coffee laced with half-breed whiskey. He gagged on the drink, remembering with vague and distant humor some of the gutslashing concoctions he'd drunk as a bum kid hanging around the hell-holes.

Seven years in a cell followed by three years of tight scrimping could sure as hell change a man's drinking habits. A laugh bubbled up out of his throat. He stared unseeing through fever-glazed eyes, his thoughts whirling, gaining speed, spinning faster like a twister across the plains, building, faster and faster, sucking him up into its swirling darkness.

XV

Shortly after midnight Jackson catfooted from his barracks and slipped into Farley's room. He stopped just inside the door, listening. Swearing softly, he grabbed the nearer figure lying on the bed, and clamped a hand over her mouth.

The woman trembled under his grip. He spoke quietly.

"Grab your clothes and get the hell outa here." She nearly fell over herself doing as she was told.

Jackson returned to the side of the bed, hoisted the mattress with a hard jerk, rolling Farley onto the floor. The little outlaw floundered about, groping in the dark for his gun, swearing obscenely all the while.

"Shut up. It's me. Where'd you pick up that damn piece of baggage?"

Farley rubbed the sleep from his eyes. "What do you care? Just some soldier's wife on her way to meet him, at least that's what she claims. Don't believe it myself." He winked, unseen by Jackson in the dark. "She was on that stage the storm held over."

"Farley, what do I have to do—set a wet-nurse after you to keep you in line? Damn you, keep out of trouble till this deal goes through. You won't be no good to me decorating the end of a wagon tongue." Abruptly Jackson changed the subject. "Did you get to see Hensen?"

"Yeah." Then he laughed. "Hensen went after it like a rattler after a rat—swallowed it whole meat. If he knew what was really cookin' in the pot . . ."

"It's up to you to see that he don't."

"He won't. Not from me anyhow." Farley paused, wishing now he hadn't had Bern change off rooms with the woman. But he was too impatient to wait for another time to hit Jackson with the question that had been curdling his insides ever since yesterday.

"Has Hensen took on any new hands?"

"No. Not that I know of."

"Then who was in the barn last night? The son-of-a-bitch creased me."

"Just a drifter slept over last night. Called himself Race Evans."

Farley snapped his fingers. "That's it! That's the bastard's name. You set him on me didn't you!"

"What? You're crazy! You don't know what the hell you're talking about."

"You'd like to think that! Listen, you're the only one could've sliced him on me. You knew we did time together."

"Quit your frothing. He pulled into Hensen's sometime yesterday afternoon, him and his horse both used up. Hensen's sister let him hole up in the barn. You sure it's the same bronc?"

"I said so, didn't I?"

Chewing on this bit of news, Jackson mentally catalogued the information for future reference. He never knew what might come in handy sometime. But to Farley he said, "You can forget about him. Hensen run him off."

"You can go to hell. You don't think I'm buying that on your say so. You put him onto me . . . I *know* it!"

"Slow down, Farley. Your cinch is getting mighty frayed far as I'm concerned. I let you off easy yesterday. I won't a second time."

Farley had outlived his usefulness as far as Maize was concerned. Right now he regretted that he hadn't approached Evans himself when he'd had the chance. If he read the drifter right, he was a fairly smart fellow who'd made some mistakes and gotten caught. But given the right kind of set-up, he'd probably carry through competently. For sure he couldn't do worse than this half-loco shorthorn.

Contempt tinged his voice as he looked down at Farley. "I'll be talking with you. But by damn, you cross me in any way, I'll slit open your gut and shit in the hole."

Leaving Farley fuming helplessly, Jackson slipped outside. The woman was waiting for him. Jackson had never given her a second thought once he dismissed her, but she had listened at the door. With the storm and all, she hadn't heard that much. For that matter, she heard very little. But more than once she'd parlayed a little knowledge into a long bluff. If there were a way to euchre a cent out of him, little Lila Garner would find it.

When Maize Jackson stepped outside, Lila sidled up to him, speaking in a deep breathy voice.

"Sounds like you and the little man have a big roast on the fire."

For all he reacted, she might have been another shadow absorbed by the storm. She pressed close against him, reaching one hand out to fondle him. "C'mon, loosen up a little. You put me out in the cold, least you can do is warm me up. Let's slip into my room so we can talk . . . and things."

His face expressionless, Jackson asked, "Where's your room?"

"Up at the main building. Might have to run Bern out. Me and him traded so I could be with Kell."

"Bern's here?" Jackson grabbed her, his nails biting into the soft flesh of her underarm beneath the woolen wrap. Lila's face scrunched up half in pain, half in fear. Too late she realized that maybe she had bought into something a little too deep for her. He squeezed her arm again.

"Yeah, he's here."

Jackson slammed her against the door next to Farley's room, reached around her to open it, then gave her another shove through the opening. He followed on her heels, gun in hand. But the room was empty.

Why the hell had Farley dragged Bern up here? The orders he'd given were to gather those beeves, closeherd them, create occasional disturbances around the ranch in keeping with Farley's original agreement with Hensen. So what the hell did he hope to gain by bringing Bern along?

Jackson regarded the frowsy woman closely. No accounting for some men's tastes, he thought with disgust. Maybe she was the best a shrimp like Farley could do. More important, just how much did she know of what was going on? No telling what kind of information that flannelmouth Farley leaked to this damn slut. Well, he'd sure as hell find out.

A half hour later the yellow-haired gunman stared dispassionately at the woman's body. She hadn't been the first woman he'd ever killed, and the way this deal was stacking, she probably wouldn't be the last. He ticked them off mentally, deriving a perverse pleasure in the accounting.

The first had been his own mother. He'd been in military school when his father—a cavalry officer—got himself killed in a New Orleans deadfall. It didn't take the grieving widow long to set herself up in business. Only difference between her and the woman at his feet was in the price they charged for their services. His mother catered only to high-ranking officers. Maize was fourteen years old when he ended his mother's career.

Next came that *puta* across the border who thought she could use her body to lure him into a trap laid for him by the *Federalistas*. Then there were a couple of squaws and their whelps he'd made into good Indians after they discovered his cache of guns and trade whiskey on the Paiute reservation near Cedar up in Utah. Was one of those skins who damn near killed him.

The last before tonight had been old lady Hensen. Once Libby nursed him back to health, the old woman urged

89

him on his way. She'd been getting more persistent, but by the time he knew enough of their affairs to realize a good thing in the making. She was in his way. He removed her.

Now this one—a bitching whore like his mother. Only one person ever got behind the emotional shell he built after he'd killed his mother—and that was Libby. Natural enough, since she saved his life. Sure, he'd been buttering up Sage, too. A good gambler coppers his bets. But he really did want Libby.

But power and wealth were *sine qua non* to him and if Libby didn't capitulate, she'd just end up in the discard pile with the rest of them.

XVI

His weight wasn't that much, but because of his height, it took all three—Sage, Libby, and Jésus—to move Race across the room to the leather settee. Once they half-carried, half-dragged him there, they hit another snag. He was too tall for the couch.

On orders from Sage, Jésus slid the couch back, giving the women enough room to build a quilt pallet on the floor by the fire.

"Sage, his head's like fire." Libby felt his forehead.

Sage came over and did the same thing, then nodded. She said to Jésus, "Strip him down."

Libby and Jésus raised their eyebrows in unison. Flushing, Sage said, "Just do it. Come on Libby, we'll need a lot more quilts."

Employing the stock home remedy for fever, she would bury Race under a mountain of feather ticks to sweat out the fever and apply cool compresses to his head to prevent convulsions.

When they returned with the quilts, Jésus spoke in hushed excitement. "Look here, señorita, señora!"

He peeled the single cover down from Race's shoulder and chest, revealing the blood-caked gash across his shoulder.

As she washed the area clean, Sage whispered, "Why didn't he tell us?" Working on him, she couldn't help but notice the man's emaciated condition. Sinew and muscle roped around his bones like ivy around an oak, little flesh filling out the spaces between. Sage had to steel herself against a rush of pity.

"There it is, Libby. What do you think?"

The flesh looked a little spongy and purple, but not necessarily infected. The fever might be the product of exposure, rather than the wound. They'd have to wait and see.

Libby helped Sage make a poultice and bandage it to his shoulder. "Sage, we'll have to watch him pretty close until his fever breaks."

"Two-hour watches all right?" Sage suggested. "I'll take the first."

Her guilt riding her hard, Sage did double duty. Each time one of the others finished standing their watch she took another turn, two watches to each of the other's one.

Thirty-six hours passed, each new hour bringing nearly another inch of snow with it, but very little change in Race. From time to time he stirred restlessly or mumbled something incoherent. But mostly he lay in a deep sleep. Several times Sage checked him just to make sure he was still breathing. Adding to her worries, there'd been no word from Josh or the crew.

The new day looked little different from its predecessor. Wind-driven snow, sleet, and more storm clouds shut out all but a bleak gray light. Curled in the rocker, Sage had difficulty keeping her eyes open.

Race's voice brought her instantly alert.

"Sage? This's real nice of you." It was a dry whisper.

Ordinarily she might have taken exception to his familiar use of her name, but right now she was too relieved that he had finally awakened.

She answered. "I'm right here. What is it?"

"This is real nice of you bringing me this soup down here."

Sage came closer and knelt beside his pallet. Although his eyes were open, they were vacant. He mumbled something about her coming to the barn alone and the soup again. He fought the covers, his naked torso glistening with sweat. She decided he was reaching the crisis point—either his fever would break or he would convulse.

He repeated her name, over and over now, almost crooning it.

As she leaned across him to tug the covers back into place, she felt the faint rhythmic undulation of his body underneath. Comprehension came slowly and when it did, she jerked back, Bull Walker's warning throbbing in her head—*Once that tiger fills his gut, it'll be the woman-hunger he'll want to feed.*

Legs folded under her, Sage sat there quietly, a little shocked at her own lack of outrage. Much as she disliked the man, his behavior couldn't be held against him under the circumstances.

But deep down was a satisfaction she refused to admit to—Race Evans had called her name, not that saloon tart Ruby Evans.

Forcing a calm she didn't feel, Sage removed the compress from the cowboy's head, dipped it in the basin of melting snow water and wrung it out. When she turned back, his eyes were open again and on her, but reason shined in them this time.

"I been dreaming." His voice was a cracked whisper.

"You're feverish." She touched the back of her hand to his forehead. "I believe it just broke." She laid the compress on his head before asking, "Can you drink some water?"

He touched tongue to dry lips before answering. "Yes, ma'am."

When Race found himself too weak to even raise his head, Sage helped him. He watched her steadily. Heads close, his eyes caught and held hers.

"Miss Hensen . . . I got to ask you . . . just now, before I woke up . . . did I say or do anything that . . . that . . ." His voice trailed off as he groped for the right way to word what he needed to find out.

Sage lowered his head to the pallet, scarlet rising from the soft curve of her throat to the golden wisps framing her face. Race had his answer. Turning his head away, he closed his eyes.

"Oh, God . . . I'm sorry," he whispered.

The next time Race awoke, Jésus was keeping watch. To Jésus' delight, the Texan spoke to him in the bastard lingo of the Mex-Tex border.

The first thing he asked was, "Are the ladies all right? Was there any more trouble?"

"They are fine, señor. No more trouble."

"What'd Hensen say when he got back and found me here?"

"*Nada,* señor. He is not back yet. None of them are. Only the four of us are here."

"Weren't you expecting them back?"

"*Sí,* but the snow must have delayed them."

Race frowned. "How long I been laid up?"

"It was two afternoons ago that you returned."

Whistling, Race absorbed that, then asked, "Anyone been taking care of the animals?"

"The ones in the barn and the *caballada.* When Señorita Hensen was not taking care of you, she was taking care of them. Maybe you are ready for some food now yourself?"

Race nodded. There were more questions he wanted to ask, but he guessed they could wait. The fire's warmth reflected off his face, engulfing him in a pleasant lethargy. By the time Libby arrived with a tray, he'd dozed off again. Setting the tray on the floor beside him, she gently shook Race awake.

"Feel up to trying a little of this?" She helped him up, but didn't need to brace him as he leaned his left shoulder against the seat of the couch.

He ate all the broth and a bite or two of the bread. There was a glass of milk on the tray and he drank all of that.

"Good Lord," he exclaimed, "I can't remember the last time I had fresh milk. That was prime!"

"Glad you liked it. Anything else I can get you? How about some books?" She reached across to the bookshelf lining the right side of the fireplace and hauled down a few well-worn books. "The crew have some dime novels in the bunkroom, if you'd rather any of those."

94

Race just smiled, shaking his head. When Libby left, he picked up one of the books. Without pictures to give him orientation, he turned the book one way, then another, unable to break the code. He could read brands and he could read tracks, but damned if he could make heads or tails out of those printed scratches.

At a sound behind him, Race twisted his head and saw Libby watching him. He hurriedly set the book down.

"I forgot to take your tray," she explained. But instead of picking it up, she came around to Race's side and looked at him. "Maize mentioned something the other night, but it took until now to register. Race, can't you read?"

Out of shame, Race had a fleeting urge to lie. Instead he admitted, "No."

"Race, would you like to learn to read while you're here?"

Excitement sparked in his eyes then filtered away. "Not much chance. Soon as Hensen gets back, he'll have me drag my freight."

"When he gets back will depend a lot on the weather, I suspect. But until then, it'll be a good way to pass time. Besides, Sage taught before she came here, you know."

"Sounds great, only . . . " he looked down at his hands. ". . . Miz Walker, I'd prefer not to bother Miss Hensen. I hope you understand." He liked Sage more than he had a right to and flaunting his ignorance before her would be a little more than his pride could handle. Besides, after that business this morning, seemed little likelihood she'd even want to bother with him.

"I think I do understand, Race. While we're on the subject," she added, as if reading his thoughts, "there's something you better understand. We don't know how long we'll be shut in, thrown together every day in the same house. You're a healthy young man and Sage is a very attractive young woman . . . "

"You don't have to say it, Miz Walker," he interrupted a little stiffly. He looked at her, wondering if Sage had said anything to her about this morning. He'd have staked his

95

saddle Sage Hensen wasn't the kind to carry tales. "You nor Miss Hensen has any cause of worry as far as I'm concerned. I had aiming my sights too high knocked the hell out of me a lot of years ago. I know my place. I won't cross the deadline."

Suddenly a boyish grin appeared on his face and he added, "But I can't guarantee my thoughts will all the time be one hundred per cent pure."

XVII

Two hours before daylight the next morning, Race wrapped one of the quilts around his middle and made his way to the bunkroom. He found and lit a lamp. The bushwhacker's clothes, laundered and mended, lay in a neat pile on one of the empty bunks. A pair of woolen socks had been slipped into the stack, an item he didn't recollect as being among the outlaw's belongings.

Jésus stirred in his bunk, so Race carried the clothes and lamp to the kitchen and dressed there. A blue enamel pot half-filled with last night's dregs sat to one side of the stove. He stirred up the fire and slid the pot over the heat. Noting the empty woodbox, Race stepped outside and carted in an armload from the dwindling supply on the porch while the coffee warmed.

He had a little appetite on him this morning but didn't feel at liberty to go rattling through the cupboards, so he contented himself with a couple of cups of the stale black brew. Then he quit the house to check the animals in the corral and barn.

Not usually one to shy off from a problem, Race realized he was dawdling, avoiding a head-to-head confrontation with Sage. He might have been feverish, but he recalled his dream all too vividly. He hadn't seen Sage since, but based on past performance . . . With a lingering sigh, he made his way back to the house.

The table was set, the good smells of cooking breakfast hitting him as Libby greeted. "Good morning!"

Race removed his hat. "Morning, ma'am. Here's some fresh milk for breakfast."

Before Libby had a chance to answer, Sage said, "Here, I'll take that. Thanks for saving me the job."

Race stared at her in astonishment. She was actually smiling at him. The one transgression he committed that she'd be justified in giving him hell about and here she was smiling at him! He shook his head in confusion. Women sure enough weren't his long suit.

"Food's ready," said Libby. "Just grab any seat, Race." They ate in the kitchen around the round oak table. The food was good and Race managed to put an appreciable amount away.

"Sure was surprised to see you up and around this morning," Libby said to him.

"No reason not to be. I was more wore out than anything." Truth was, he wasn't as strong as he'd thought and he came to breakfast with honest relief, welcoming a legitimate excuse to get off his unsteady legs for a while.

There were more chores to be done around the ranch and Race was the only man around to do them, so he solicited information from the other three.

"Do you have any supply of wood around here?"

"There's a stack of rounds behind the dog pen. Most of the split wood burned out that night you spent in the barn," Sage told him.

"You got a maul?"

None of them knew what a maul was, but they expected whatever wood-cutting tools Hensen had would be lying out with the pile of wood.

His next big concern was the cattle. If Hensen were snowed in somewhere, the untended cattle would drift before the storm. Last winter up in Wyoming they had had a big freeze and die-up. Race himself had found a bunch of cattle that had piled up against a drift fence. The lead cattle, unable to advance, went under the crush of animals

98

drifting up from behind, forming a bridge of frozen flesh. And, if Race was any judge, this winter was shaping up to make that one look like Indian summer by contrast.

As he plied his questions, he drew mental pictures of the numbers and distribution of Hensen's stock, the general lay of the land beyond what he already knew, where lines of deciduous and evergreen trees provided natural buffers, locations of salting grounds, fences, watering holes.

The pictures he got from the information gleaned were pitifully inadequate. Apparently Hensen shared none of the ranch's workings with the women in spite of their interest. Now his herds would suffer because of it.

"One last thing. Do you know if there are any good snow hosses in the remuda?"

They didn't know that, either. Race spoke, almost to himself. "Well, from what I've seen of the cavvy, that long-legged claybank of the gulcher's looks as good a bet as any. I'll use it and his rigging."

Sage opened her mouth as if to say something, but withheld. The now familiar look of contempt was back on her face as she rose and left the table.

With Jésus helping as much as he was able, Race spent the rest of the morning splitting and carting wood to the porch. After lunch he slapped Stubbs' double-rigged Texas saddle on the claybank. Before he traded down to that old rimfire hull, this was the kind of rigging he'd always used himself.

Race wasn't sure what he expected to accomplish riding out into the storm, except maybe to pick up some sign of Hensen's herds. Even that seemed unlikely, all things considered. But he was too much of a cowboy not to make the try.

Taking a fix on the direction of the storm, he set out. The wind against his cheek was a poor guide, but the only one he had, with the air like frozen buttermilk and vision under ten yards.

Just an hour's searching told Race he wasn't up to the rugged physical demands he was placing on himself, so he decided to pack it in for the day. No sooner had he made the decision than a ghost-frosted figure emerged from the storm astride a long-limbed horse.

Lifting his hand to hail the man, he cut the motion short when he saw the rifle across the other's knees. The stranger gave no sign and rode straight at Race in a slow and indomitable way.

Race kneed the claybank aside to keep from being ridden down. Something he saw made him reach out and grab the near rein of the other man's horse.

A web of hoarfrost curtained the man's unseeing eyes. Race tried to lift the man's rifle, but it was frozen solid to the man's hands, just as the man himself was frozen to his saddle. Race swallowed back a rush of gorge. Shaking out a loop, he roped the stranger's horse, took a couple of dallies around his horn with the other end of the rope.

He stopped dead—cocked his head, listening. He heard it again—the bawl of drifting cattle. The storm was heading them this way.

With his grisly burden on lead, Race began a tight circle of the cattle. When he finished, he estimated the count between eight and nine hundred. From what he understood, Hensen only ran around 1600 head.

How come to be so many in one bunch? he wondered. That was contrary to the ways of cattle on range as open as this plateau, unless they'd been gathered. And Hensen sure enough wouldn't be holding roundup this late in the season.

Had the dead man been riding herd, trying to stop the drift? Or was his horse just moving along instinctively with the other animals? Race checked the man's horse for a brand but there was none. The one Race was riding had none either. Could there be some kind of connection?

Hell, he told himself, I ain't no damn Texas Ranger. Just a drifting bum with borrowed clothes on my back and a borrowed kak under my seat.

Before he hit back for the ranch, he had one more chore. On circle he'd run across a few calves frozen into the mud where they'd been standing. No way to free them short of butchering off their legs. Trouble was, they were still alive.

A half-starved wolf was tearing at one of the bawling calves and others were closing in when Race found them. Elsewhere throughout the herd he found steers who'd torn off their hooves trying to paw through the frozen crust to the graze beneath. Still others were down with lung fever.

By the time Race finished, the barrel of Stubbs' Winchester burned hot in his hands.

XVIII

While Pipe Spring provided an oasis in this bitter high desert country, the fort itself was something less than a palace of pleasure. A couple dozen Mormon men, women, and children normally worked and lived there. But the storm brought nearly that many in the shape of stranded travelers who kept dribbling in the first few days of the storm.

That many people on varying backgrounds crowded together in such a small area was bound to cause problems for Pulsipher, the fort's superintendent. And it did.

Tension was already high after discovery of the woman's body. Rumor had it she got drunk and fell and cracked her skull. But Pulsipher noted the finger bruises on her upper arms and warned off his people. They'd share food and accommodations with the outsiders, but otherwise leave them to their own devices.

The outsiders brought in liquor and idled most of the time away playing cards in the meeting room. Fights were common and became more violent with each passing day. But Pulsipher wasn't the only one whose concern grew daily. Lin and Bandy had their doubts about the way things were breaking, too.

"Lin, I just gotta tell somebody or bust! I seen Farley go off with that woman before she got sent to hell on a shutter. But that don't bother me half so much as something else I seen—the other night when they figgered no one was looking, I saw the boss slip some hard gold into Farley's hand."

Lin whistled softly. "Better go easy there, pard. Talk like that can buy you a one-way ticket to hell."

"I know it. But I swear to God it's true. I've been worrying on that. I told myself they couldn't help but rub elbows, things so crowded here. But they always make out like they're hostile or avoiding each other when someone's watching. I mean I seen Farley, heads together with Jackson.

"But just tell me what the hell business the boss could have with Farley, that he'd be paying him hard cash, especially if Farley's been behind all the boss' troubles like he claims. Why didn't he just cut loose on the little bastard on sight? Don't make no sense!"

Lin nodded thoughtfully. "I don't know what to say, Bandy. Ever since we come to this place, I've had a bad feeling. Like sometimes I can just smell gunsmoke. Tell you one thing—anytime you herd men together like a bunch of penned cows, a head of steam's just natcherally gonna build till the lid blows off. You watch—we're in for three kinds of hell before this storm blows over."

Almost in response to his prediction, a chair grated back roughly and toppled over. Walker teetered near the table he just pushed away from.

"What do you mean my paper's no good! You with that damn freezeout cleaned me out of pocket money. How'm I gonna play?"

Jackson shrugged. "Greenhorns got no business playing over their heads."

Bull Walker swore. "I never welshed on a bet yet. No reason for you not to take my marker. I got a right to win some of my own money back. Damn freezeout's all you know. Don't have guts enough to try something else."

"Takes more guts than you got to play freezeout. You're either a winner or a loser. Time you faced up to the fact there can be only one winner, but lots of losers. You're a loser, Bull. Swallow it and leave me alone."

Jackson rose and walked away. After promoting a new bottle from somewhere, he returned to his table. Walker was still sitting there.

103

Grunting in annoyance, Jackson toed a chair out and sat down. After he poured himself a drink, he shoved the bottle toward Walker.

"A game of showdown, Jackson. You name the stakes."

"Look, Bull, I'm only going to beat you and there's no way I can spend a damn I.O.U. Only paper you got that might interest me would be your share of the 3-H spread."

That caught Walker cold. "That's Libby's. I ain't got no claim on it."

"That aint the way you were telling it the other night. It's put-up or shut-up time, Bull."

"Yeah, well what've you got to put up against it?"

Jackson dug into his shirt pocket, tossed a roll onto the table. "Couple of thousand there."

"Hell, a third share of the outfit is easily worth twice that."

The gunman shrugged, gathered up the bills and pocketed them, laughing. "What'd you say about guts? Figured you'd crawfish when the chips were down."

"Who said anything about crawfishing! What'll it be? Seven-card showdown?" With a borrowed pencil stub, Walker labored out a rough I.O.U.

"Well, Walker, we get in any kind of involved play, you'll claim I cold-decked you, then I'll have to shoot you to 'protect my honor.' You wanted a guts play, I'll give you one plus all the odds."

Jackson called out, "Anyone got a new deck?"

One of the other stranded travelers handed him a box, the seal unbroken. Sensing some excitement to break the monotony, others in the room began crowding around the little table.

"All right, Bull, here it is." He laid the unopened box in front of Walker. "I'll never touch the cards. You open the box, shuffle them all you want. Then deal the three top cards. I'm betting you this wad," he again withdrew the roll from his pocket and slapped it on the table, "against that piece of paper that one of those three cards you deal will be a jack, an ace, or a four. If that sounds like a fair bet, why you just pick up that deck and start peeling."

Walker took a moment to think. Three cards out of a deck of fifty-two—fifty-four if he left the jokers in. And Jackson was betting one would be a jack, ace, or four. Odds sounded good all right. Too damn good. For Jackson to lay a bet like that, there just had to be a skunk buried somewhere in that woodpile.

But if he backed down now, everybody there'd mark him down as a fourflusher. Besides, there was the off-chance that Jackson's bet was on the level. He'd sure like to line his pockets with that wad of Jackson's.

Bull scooped up the box, ran his fingernail under the seal and opened it. Jackson probably was depending on the sequence of the new deck, somehow. He'd make damn good and sure he broke that sequence.

Slowly he riffled and re-riffled the deck, split them, and ran them through each other. He did this at least a half dozen times before finishing off with what the cowboys called a "Hindu shuffle."

Once he satisfied himself that he scrambled the sequence, Bull cautiously raised the top card and turned it over.

Three of spades.

An involuntary sigh escaped his lips. In spite of the poorly heated room, Walker was sweating. He rubbed his deal hand on the side of his pants before lifting the next card. Setting his hand on the deck, he peeled back the corner of the next card and broke into a relieved smile.

King of hearts. One more to go.

With building confidence, Bull slipped the third card over. His eyes spread wide, staring at it as if by doing so he could change it.

Savagely, Walker slapped Jackson's bottle to the floor and elbowed his way out of the room.

A half-smile quirked Jackson's mouth as he held the third card up for the others to see—

Four of clubs!

As Maize Jackson tucked the money and Walker's paper back into his shirt, he smiled to himself. On the face of it, chances of pulling out one of the named cards were three in fifty-four. Closer look showed that with four suits and two jokers, it'd be lowered to little better than three in twelve, still not bad odds. But what it actually came down to—and Jackson tried it enough times to know—was that seven out of ten times you would draw any three cards named.

A clamor and a woman's scream just outside sent all the men racketing to the door. Jackson pushed his way through to the front.

Pulsipher and his second-in-command stood unarmed, facing a gun-waving and slightly drunk Kell Farley.

"What's going on?" Jackson demanded.

A man at his shoulder said, "That bronc cornered one of them Mormon women and laid a hand on her. When Pulsipher and his man called him on it, he pulled his iron."

"You Mormons hog all the women for yourself." Farley's speech came thick and slurred.

Fury raged in Jackson. He stepped between the two Mormons and Farley. "Lay up that gun. You're drunk and you've insulted one of their ladies."

Jackson had his walnut-butted gun in his hand. Farley was too erratic a little bugger for Maize to take chances with him.

But drunk and erratic, Farley wasn't crazy. He remembered his last go-round with Jackson. Plus the cold shock of seeing him there with his iron unsheathed and pointed at his belly went a long way toward sobering up the little outlaw fast.

He holstered his gun. "Just funning a little. The g'damn place is so dead, just thought I'd liven things a little. No harm." He rubbed the back of his hand across his mouth, then staggered out the open gates toward the barracks. Inside he fumed. Jackson just added more fuel to an already burning hate.

Jackson watched him go. To Pulsipher he said, "Sorry this happened, but you know he's not one of Rafter 3-H men." Mentally he thanked the stars that Hensen hadn't seen the incident. If he got to thinking too much, he might call off his deal with Farley and all the groundwork Jackson laid would go to hell.

He realized suddenly that Pulsipher was studying his

106

face. With a nod he returned to the meeting room.

Pulsipher's segundo spoke first. "Woe unto them that rise up early in the morning that they may follow strong drink,' " he quoted from Isaiah.

But Pulsipher just grunted. "Tell you the truth, Orem, I'm less worried about their drinking than what they'll be like once they start running out of the damn stuff."

XIX

Race drew at the hitch-rail in front of the house, feeling as cold and stiff as the frozen corpse behind him. Before he had the reins tied, Sage was at his side. An unfamiliar warmth stole through the cowboy—she'd been waiting, watching for him to return.

She confirmed this by asking, "Are you all right? We were beginning to worry."

Nodding, Race tugged on the rope stretched out from his saddle to the horse behind. Sage's breath caught as she saw the stiff, upright burden.

"Is he . . . did you—"

He shook his head. "Found him froze to death. Best I could tell, he'd been riding herd on your cows. Thought he might be one of your brother's men."

"Is that why you brought him here?"

"No . . . figured I might need a change of clothes," he retorted with bleak humor.

Pursing her lips into a wry grin, Sage muttered, "*Touché.*"

He didn't know what the word meant, but from the expression on her face, he gathered he'd won a temporary truce.

"I've got about an hour and a half of working light yet. There's a bunch of cows headed this way, the storm pushing them. Unless they find food and shelter, they'll keep traveling—fences or nothing will stop them, not even that Big Canyon.

"Saw a pretty thick stand of pine a couple hundred yards back. I figure if Jésus can help me, we might be able to haul enough feed to hold them for tonight, or at least slow 'em down. Don't know for sure that it'll work, but about half your herd is strung out back there and we ought to try to save what we can.''

Sage nodded. Race hadn't anticipated help from the women, but both Sage and Libby pitched right in alongside him and Jésus. Race quickly hitched a couple of tough little Morgans to the two hay sleds. As soon as one sled was loaded, he and Jésus drove it to the copse while the women forked loose hay onto the other one.

The four strained without a break, only giving in when it became too cold and too dark to work effectively. But by this time, the first of the cows found the feed.

That evening after picking at a cold supper, they lounged at the table, too worn to get up. The day's efforts showed most on Race, whose face was drawn and pale.

Libby said, "Sage prepared your first lesson and I thought we'd begin tonight, Race. But I can see you've about had it for today."

"Why hell, no!" He blurted. "If it's all the same to you, Miz Walker, I'd sure enough like to start now . . . unless you're too done in your ownself."

Sage offered, "If you want to help him, Lib, Jésus and I'll clean up."

"Okay. Cowboy, wait right here." In a few minutes Libby returned with paper, pen and ink, a picture catalogue and a few simple books. She spread them out on the kitchen table and read off their titles.

"Any you'd prefer to start with?" she asked.

Thinking of his mother's only Book, he answered without hesitation, "The Bible." That wasn't one of the books on the table.

A look flashed between Sage and Libby. Misinterpreting the exchange, the redfaced cowboy said, "Guess I jammed my hoof in my mouth again. If you think it'd be wrong for a man like me to use the Good Book . . . ."

"No. Of course not," they hastened to assure him. Sage said, "Use mine. It's right there on the shelf behind you."

For a solid week the four followed the same routine—carrying feed during the day, working at night.

Jésus was the first to give out after the third day.

The weather worsened and by the fifth day Race refused to let the women help outside any longer. By the eleventh day he had to give it up himself. From that point on, the range stock would have to fend for themselves, survive any way they could.

During the days they worked together Sage discovered that whatever Race lacked in formal education was more than compensated by native intelligence and plain dogged work. A salty wit offset his usual gravity and he wasn't above the cowboy credo of playing practical jokes. Sage smiled remembering the hours Libby spent looking for a "left-handed hammer" for him before finally catching on.

His pride wasn't the overbearing kind, it was undergirded by a genuine humbleness. But the thing that amused her the most about him was his drawl. For the most part he was easy going, but on those occasions when something did rile him, his South Texas drawl broadened in almost comic proportion to his anger.

One time, a six-week-old bummer calf he'd just hand fed caught him bending over and butted him head over haunches into a pile of snow. While Race was face down in the snow, the 125-pound calf climbed on his back and stood there bawling.

Unaware of Sage's presence, Race finally extricated himself and in strong language told that calf what he thought of its intelligence, ingratitude and dubious ancestry, each word stringing out longer as he built up a head of steam.

That was one occasion Sage was too busy laughing to be offended by the cowboy's swearing. Race turned quickly, face reddening as he realized she'd been watching him. Like a rain over the desert, his anger evaporated.

The better she got to know Race, the better she liked him. And this worried her. As democratic as the West claimed to be, rigid barriers nevertheless existed. A rancher's daughter never associated with cowboys. And Race Evans wasn't even a common cowboy, but an ex-convict.

110

More and more frequently she had to remind herself of that fact.

As for Race, with the deep snows and sub-zero weather locking them in, he turned all his energies into his studies. After a rough start when he figured he was too much of a hollowhorn to learn anything, the damnable code finally broke and he caught on like a torch to a haystack.

Things cracked right along with him reading everything in sight. There were quiet moments, too, in his bunk at night when he'd lean back and dream his private dreams. A full four weeks had passed since the day he first set foot on Rafter 3-H Connected. Race had the kitchen table staked out and Sage and Libby were doing handwork in the living room.

"He's really changed a lot, hasn't he?" Sage asked.

"Who, Race?"

"Um-huh."

"Tell you the truth, Sage, I don't think he's changed so much as your perception of him has."

"That could well be true. Remember the first day? He really had me spitting fire. Then the next day when he returned and put on that dead man's clothes while they were still warm just made my stomach churn over. Far as I was concerned, Race Evans was the bottom of the pile—a dirty jailbird and rootless drifter parading around in a dead man's clothes . . ."

At Libby's sharp intake of breath, Sage pulled around.

Race stood in the archway between the rooms, a stack of books in his arm. From the stricken look on his face, it was a cinch-bet he'd caught the tail end of Sage's remarks. Flushing with embarrassment he said, "I . . . Miz Walker, you told me to bring these books in here when I finished. I sure enough didn't mean to barge in on you ladies. I'll put 'em away later."

He spun on one heel, sought out the refuge of the bunkroom. Dumping the books on an empty bunk, he walked to the room's single window, leaned a forearm against the frame and stared unseeing at the frosted glass.

Damn but his insides felt empty. He didn't expect Sage to feel anything like he felt for her, but he'd been so sure she'd gotten over the old contempt for him. Maybe that'd just been wishful thinking on his part.

And when it came right down to push for shove, her opinion nor anyone else's could change the things he'd done or been. Hell, for that matter what was he now? He couldn't even claim the dignity of being a hired hand. Just a bum working off his keep. Hell, he couldn't blame her.

Sage had followed and now as she watched Race from the doorway, and unfamiliar sensation sent warm sparks ricocheting through her. Joining him at the window, she laid a hand on his arm.

"Race . . ."

His muscles went rigid under her touch. She felt the electric shock go through him as he pulled stiffly erect.

"I'm not sure how much you heard in there . . ."

Forcing a grin that didn't quite make it, he turned to face her.

"Why, it don't matter, Miss Hensen."

"Maybe not to you, but it does to me. I was telling Libby how much my impressions of you changed since you first came here. I don't know why, but all of a sudden it's very important to me that you understand that."

Even though he tried not to read more into it than she intended, her words sent another electric tremor through him, so vibrant even Sage felt it. The silence built in the charged air.

He lifted one hand and gently touched her face. His expression softened as he ran a finger across the cartilage bump on her nose, the only flaw in an otherwise perfect face. More than anything he wanted to draw her into his arms.

Something in his look telegraphed his intent and Sage, confused by her own feelings, took a backward step. She spoke hurriedly, breaking the moment.

"Christmas eve is two nights from now. I . . . Libby and I have a little celebration planned. We'd like you and Jésus to share the evening with us."

Anticipation rode high in Race the next couple of days. Until now, one day pretty much followed another. For the first time in his life he looked forward to a holiday. And while he tried not to make too much of the invitation, he still felt nimble-blooded as a colt on spring pasture.

That afternoon he spoke to Jésus with affectionate courtesy, "Tío, tonight we celebrate the coming of the holy day with the ladies, and I need a favor off you."

"*Cuál es?*"

"Well, my face looks like the wrong end of a sheep. I'd sure enough consider it a favor if you'd loan me your razor."

"You are welcome to anything of mine, *Raza*. Do you need to ask?"

"Sometimes that damn stiff-necked Texas pride of mine gets in the way. *Lo siento.*"

Jésus understood what a difficult thing it was for a Texan to be obligated to a Mexican. But the cowboy's admission and simple apology buried prejudices and bonded their friendship.

After Race shaved, the old man further obliged him by trimming his shaggy mane. The cowboy capped off these preliminary preparations with a luxury he enjoyed almost daily since his stay—a soak in a tub of hot soapy water.

When he finished his bath, he dumped his clothes in the used water and scrubbed them. While they dried strung over various pieces of furniture near the potbellied stove, Race stretched out on his bunk in a state of pure contentment.

He'd been ready an hour before the women finally called them to supper. With a final check in front of the cracked mirror, he adjusted the knot on his neck-scarf muttering, "Evans, you look damn near human."

Supper was the best he'd ever eaten, the women having worked wonders with an old gobbler he'd shot the day before. He left himself open for some good natured ribbing as he took thirds of everything on the table.

In a quiescent mood, they moved to the fire. Sage stared at Race, marveling at his appearance tonight. The hollows

113

in his cheeks had filled out, the fever blisters were gone. The blue silk scarf lent him by Jésus intensified the blue of his eyes. Shaved and curried that way, he owned a rugged good looks.

When Race caught her watching him, she spoke hurriedly, a note of wistfulness in her voice. "This is the first Christmas I've ever had without—" she started to say *without my parents,* but fearful of dampening the mood changed it to, "—without a Christmas tree."

Race's tone matched hers as he said, "This is the first Christmas I've ever had, period."

"Hey," Libby said, "before you two get too moody, I think it's time for this." She pulled out a hamper and withdrew packages from it. Wishing Sage a Merry Christmas she handed her a package. Sage in turn pulled out a ribbon-wrapped present from under the couch.

The two women opened their packages and held up nearly identical pink shawls each had crocheted for the other.

Laughing, Libby said, "What is it philosophers say about great minds running in the same track?"

Then they exchanged gifts with Jésus. Pride clear in his face, he handed them each silver crosses inlaid with bits of polished turquoise that he'd fashioned himself. In exchange he received a couple of silk kerchiefs from Sage and a woolen muffler from Libby.

Race sat quietly back, enjoying his role as spectator. Libby startled him as she held out a package to him.

"Merry Christmas, Race." Sage handed him a bundle, too. That was the first time she had ever called him by his first name.

Suppressed excitement caused his hand to move awkwardly as he gingerly undid the ribbons from Libby's gift. Inside was a muffler—except for the color, a twin to the one she'd made for Jésus.

Then he opened the package from Sage. In it was her Bible, the only one Libby had used to teach him from. He fingered it with trembling hands, unable to look up at Sage.

"You ladies . . ." he started to say, but an unfamiliar

burning sensation constricted the back of his throat, cutting off his words. Helplessly he shook his head.

"Well, it's late," Libby said. "We'd better get to bed."

"Wait. I want you to know this has been the best . . . nobody ever . . . I just wish I could keep these things you all gave me."

"Why can't you?" Sage and Libby asked simultaneously.

"Well, I didn't know . . . I don't have nothing to give you in return."

"We didn't expect anything, Race. Besides, you've given us some of yourself every day you've been here," said Libby. Sage didn't say anything, but she nodded in agreement.

Lifting his hands, Race looked to Jésus.

The old man laughed. "Don't look to me, *amigo*. Just keep in mind what we talked about this evening."

Race knew he was referring to his "stiffnecked Texas pride." Nodding he said, "Then I'll just say thank you both. This's been the best day of my life and I just wish it never had to end."

But as Race returned to the bunkroom, he knew it wouldn't last forever and there'd probably never be another like it.

XX

Later that night after everyone had bedded down, Race took a lantern and a block of stinkers and slipped outside. He crunched across the snow to the woodpile, got the axe and headed into the woods that rimmed the area.

After some floundering about, he found what he'd been looking for—a well-proportioned cedar tree close to eight feet high. Chopping the tree close to its base, he carried it to the barn, where he scrounged up a couple of boards and a ten-inch iron spike. Using the ax-blade like an adze, he evened off the bottom of the cedar, notched the boards, and fashioned a crude but serviceable stand.

A glimmer of anticipation ran through him as he carried the tree to the house, where he managed to get it through to the living room without knocking anything over.

Working by the dim light of the smouldering fire, Race shoved aside one of the leather chairs to make room, setting the tree midway between the formal parlor and the dining room.

At a whisper of sound behind him, Race wheeled around. Sage stood there, the scattergun gripped tightly in her hands.

After a moment of startled silence, Race began to laugh. "You're bound to get me with that thing yet!"

"You're the one who told me to keep it handy at all times, after that bushwhacker cornered us. If you get shot, it's no one's fault but your own, Mr. Evans."

"You called me Race earlier this evening," he reminded.

"Did I?" But before he could answer, Sage asked, "What are you doing anyway?"

When he showed her, her face lit up, delighted as any kid. "A Christmas tree?"

He nodded.

"Will you help me decorate it? Tonight?"

"You bet! What do I do?"

"First, we have to pop some corn."

While Sage went into the other room to get the popper and a jar of dried corn, Race raked up the coals in the fireplace and added fresh logs. In half an hour, the wooden dough tray brimmed with exploded kernels.

"Now what?"

Sage threaded a needle and handed it to him. "Just run this through the popcorn and slide the corn down to the knot." His big hand were better suited for stitching saddle leather and an involuntary "damn" escaped every time he crumbled one of the delicate puffs.

Finally he gave it up altogether, content just to sit back and watch Sage's nimble fingers at work. This was the first time he'd ever seen her with her hair loose. It hung like a golden cape to her waist. Little white moccasins showed under the full wrapper she wore made of some soft fluffy material.

"Prettier'n a sego lily," he murmured.

Sage looked up at him. "What did you say?"

He shook his head. "Just talking to myself."

"Don't tell me you're through threading your popcorn already!"

He shook his head again, a grin spreading across his face.

"Ate all mine."

Sage laughed outright at that. "The way you went at the food tonight, I can believe it. All right, if you're given up on this job, how about making a star for the top of the tree. Any good Texan ought to be able to do that."

"A good Texan, maybe. All I can guarantee is that I'm a Texan."

Race rustled up a chunk of softwood and a paring knife. Before settling down to his whittling, he fed the fire again.

When in his shadowed life had he ever known such contentment?

Some quiet moments passed before Sage spoke. "Race, do you have any family?"

He frowned thoughtfully before answering. "None to speak of. Might have some brothers and sisters around somewhere, but I don't know for sure."

"Race is such an unusual name, I was just wondering if it were a family name or a nickname."

"Just a nickname." He grinned remembering. "Ruby tagged me with it. You might remember that night down to the barn I mentioned Ru—"

Sage stiffened, interrupted abruptly. "I really don't think we should discuss her."

"Him," Race corrected.

"But I thought . . ."

"Ruby was a nigg—a Nigro gambler. Caught me with my hand in his pocket. I took off hell-for-leather, but he jumped some cowboy's hoss and rode me down. Never been so scared in my life—'cept for that day I almost shot you. You can imagine what was running through a Texan kid's mind with a six-foot-four reconstruction Nigro after him. I ran so fast, I beat the hoss out—for a while, anyhow. Took a catch-rope to bring me down. Lordy, I thought sure he was going to kill me, but he burst out laughing. He figured all that energy could be put to better use. So instead of beating hell out of me or turning me over to the law, he teamed up with me."

Race told her about his stint as a "two-legged race hoss."

"When that deal busted up, he rode out of his way to deposit me with a friend of his in West Texas. Burr Hazeltine—he rodded an outfit in that country. Ruby introduced me as Race Evans. Tagging me with his last name was a sample of his sense of humor. But what the hell, my own name wasn't one I was particular proud of, so I let it lay."

"Did you stay on with this Hazeltine?"

"You bet. Till then I was just another punk kid heading straight to hell. Took odd jobs when I could find them,

118

stole when I couldn't." He felt color creep into his face at the admission, but it wasn't in him to lie to this girl.

"You really enjoy working cattle, don't you?"

"Sure. Like snapping broncs even better. I rode the rough-string for Swan." He said it with unconscious pride. A bronc-peeler was considered a cut above an ordinary puncher. They earned more, too. That was Sage's next question.

He nodded. "Ordinarily that's the way it works, but not in my case." He explained, "You see, when I got out . . ." he faltered, feeling the heat of shame, then plunged on, ". . . when I got out of the pen, I was hard to put for a job. Pretty much like now. But at Swan, Singhaus agreed to take me on at two-thirds pay. On the books I was collecting thirty a month and found, but actually I only got twenty. Singhaus pocketed the other ten.

"Then when I took over the rough string, I picked up thirty a month with Singhaus skimming off fifteen. It wasn't easy, but in the three years I worked there, I managed to save up enough to buy that little buskskin broodmare. Hoped to start a little outfit of my own some day, maybe over in Nevada or here in Arizona."

"Race, what happened between that last cattle drive and your starting work for Swan?"

"I guess you know, Miss Hensen," he answered quietly. "You read that letter."

"But—were you really guilty?"

"Hell, yes!" Race took a knick out of his thumb with the knife as he said it. With a murmured *Damn*! he lifted the cut to his mouth.

"But why?"

Race flushed deeply. "I wanted to get married."

Sage was silent a long moment. "I'm sorry. I didn't mean to pry."

Race surprised himself by saying, "I don't mind talking about it if you don't mind listening."

"I would like to know."

"I was just shy of eighteen, but I'd done a man's work most of my life. From the time I took on regular with Hazeltine, I salted away a dollar here and there against the

119

day I could stake my own outfit. I'd never really been a kid and didn't much think like one. At seventeen I was ready to settle down. All I'd ever wanted was a home of my own and a good woman to share it with.

"You might find this hard to believe, but to a man like me, a good woman's more precious than life-giving water. But a man like me don't often get a chance to meet with decent women. At trail's end of that third drive, I met Jen . . and she was a good girl."

"She let me court her, but she wouldn't let me tell her daddy. He was a respectable town-man and I was just a common drover. Hoping to sort of make up the difference, I pulled all my savings together and made a down payment on a little spread nearby. It was small and unstocked, but something solid to build on. I hired a trail pard of mine to go mavericking with me on shares. Mavericking hadn't been outlawed yet in Wyoming.

"Will and me put in sixteen, eighteen hours a day, every day. But mavericks wasn't plentiful like back home. Oh, we made some headway, but Jen was getting almighty impatient."

"Race, did your—your fianceé have any idea what you were doing?"

He lifted his hands in a meaningless gesture, but didn't answer. *Sure Jen knew. Hell, it was her idea.* He was patient, young with a lot of good years ahead of him and willing to wait. But confronted with her ultimatum, he buckled in to her demands.

Continuing, Race said, "Will and me weren't greedy. The outfits would never have even noticed their losses except for a piece of bad luck.

"A kid wrangler after a mare that quit his cavvy run smack into us. When he saw what was going on, he pulled iron and started throwing lead every which way. Trouble was, his own hoss was gunshy and started humping through our gather. All that commotion choused up the beeves, set them to running. Meantime, the kid's hoss dumped him in the middle of that mess.

"When I saw what happened, I spurred back to pick him up before he got trampled. I managed that, but it was too late. The fall broke his neck. Him and me was about the same age, but he was a kid.

"By this time, the whole camp was down on us. They invited Will to a mid-air dance. Only reason I didn't get strung up, too, was because one of their crew saw what I'd tried to do for their jingler. They turned me over to the law."

"What happened to Jen?"

Race laughed without rancor. "Like I said, she was a good girl. If it come out she'd been mixing with me, it would've spoilt her reputation. Word got to me while I was waiting trial that her daddy announced her engagement to some son-of-a-bi—uh, banker or something."

"I'm sorry, Race."

He smiled at her. "I was sorry, too, at the time. Here you go." He handed her the whittled-out star.

Sage eyes it critically. Straight-faced she said, "I guess I've seen worse, but I can't remember where or when."

A glance in Race's direction showed him sober-faced. She'd just been skylarking him. Had he taken offense?

"There's something," he said, "about Kell Farley." He'd gone this far, he decided not to hold anything back from her. "Farley and me were cell-mates up at Laramie. For about a year, until they transferred him out to Nebraska."

A shock of disappointment went through Sage. So he had lied that first day.

"I wanted you to know. But so help me God, it wasn't till the next morning when I caught him setting fire to the barn I knew for sure it was the same Farley. It'd been a good five years since I last saw him."

He watched her intently, trying to gauge her reaction. The tension washed out of him when she said in a warm voice, "Thanks for telling me, Race. Let's finish the tree."

Together they draped the tree with the popcorn strands. Upending a cylinder of firewood, Race climbed aboard and fitted the reamed-out hole at the bottom of the star onto the top center branch of the cedar.

Hopping down, he asked, "How's it look, boss-lady?"

"Terrible!" But she was laughing as she said it.

He stepped back by her to take a look. The tree wasn't dead center to begin with. The added weight of the whittled star caused the whole top to list miserably to one side.

"Don't look so bad to me," he defended, but he was laughing, too.

Hands on her hips, she said, "Leave it to a man. Here, I'll fix it."

As Race handed her up onto the stump, Sage again felt that galvanizing shock go through the cowboy. Hurriedly she withdrew her hand from his.

With his boots on, Race stood nearly a foot taller than Sage. At this height disadvantage, Sage struggled just to reach the bottom of the star.

Race watched, trying to keep a straight face. Each unsuccessful attempt she made to right the tree, his grin spread a little wider. This wasn't lost on Sage and made her only that much more determined to get the darned thing straight. In desperation she leaned her full weight against the bow of the tree. Its brittle mainstem snapped, sweeping her off her precarious perch.

Race reached out to break her fall. As he caught her, her weight drove his unyielding knee back against the edge of the overstuffed chair. He toppled backwards carrying Sage with him and onto his lap.

His voice carried protective concern as he asked, "Are you all right? Did you hurt yourself?"

But Sage was laughing. "Only thing I hurt was my pride."

Something in Race's expression choked off her laughter. Tentatively he drew her closer and laid a gentle kiss on her lips. When she didn't resist, a surging hope tore through him.

"Oh God, Sage," He pulled her hard against him, closed his lips over hers in savage hunger.

All the years of loneliness and shattered dreams fired that kiss. His fierceness triggered a primitive response from Sage. But some small part of her mind held back, alerting her to the dangers of the unexplored ground she was treading.

Fears of her own raw feelings spurred her. With a violence born of passion she suddenly jerked free and slapped him, the blow crackling like a gunshot in the room's stillness.

Race sat still a long moment, an embarrassed flush gradually swallowing the imprint left on his face by her hand.

"I'm sorry . . . I had no right . . ."

"No you didn't, you—" she hesitated, groping for a word, "—you *tiger*!"

Race blanched, the epithet hitting him with more impact than the slap, dredging up all the old shame of his checkered past.

As he rose from the chair, the imprint of her hand was again clean on his face. A fleeting fear gripped Sage as he loomed above her. But he didn't touch her—just looked, unable to hide the misery deep inside.

Finally he said, "That's a word you people use kind of free around here. I take it you know what it means?"

Like a prairie dog mesmerized by a rattlesnake, she stared at him then slowly shook her head. She'd heard Bull call him that and the word just blurted out.

"You ever seen a picture of a tiger?" he asked. "You know what they look like—where they're kept?" He nodded as he saw the change in her expression. "Now you got it. Tigers are animals—animals with stripes. Damn dangerous animals that have to be kept locked up in iron cages with bars.

"Well, lady, I wish to hell I could say you named me wrong. For a minute there I forgot I'm just a jailbird. A *tiger* that crawled out of his cage and crossed the deadline. But if you've got an ounce of honesty in you, you'll admit I had some help in doing it.

"Good night, Miss Hensen and . . ." he added with bitter irony, " . . . Merry Christmas."

XXI

Pulsipher's prediction wasn't far off. Trouble increased in inverse proportion to the amount of liquor being circulated. As the supply diminished nerves frayed and tempers snapped.

Hensen walked over to Walker and sniffed the concoction his segundo had been guzzling.

"My God," this stuff'd make a jack-rabbit raise on its haunches and spit in a wolf's eye. You better pull yourself together, Bull. You been lapping up hogwash ever since Maize froze you out."

"Froze me out hell . . ."

Hensen gave the man a look of disgust. "Don't remember no one twisting your arm behind your back."

"That ain't the point, dammit! I been slickered by a gunhung sharper and I aint gonna let is stand."

"Don's see where you got no choice."

"I got a choice and so do you, Josh."

"How do you figger I got anything to do with it?"

"You just think about it. With me eased out of the picture, who's your new pardner? Jackson, that's who!"

"Like hell he is."

"Like you just told me, I don't see where you got no choice—unless we throw our chips together."

"You got something particular in mind?"

"I sure as hell do. Neither of us can match cutters with Jackson, but both of us together can."

"Listen, Bull, I draw the line at bushwhacking."

"I'm not talking about bushwhacking. We'll take him on fair. He's a card-sharp and a cheat—our problem is proving it. We can't, but if we pull him into a game and both call him, it's the word of both of us against his. He'll draw—he'll have to. Only thing is, he'll be whipsawed between us."

Hensen rubbed his hand across his forehead. Walker's idea was so jack-ass simple it just might work. If he let Bull carry the action, Maize would be concentrating on him. Hell, he might get rid of both of them at the same time.

"I'm in," he said.

Bern was an unknown quantity to Hensen and Walker—just another stranded traveler so far as they knew. They had kept their conversation low and confidential, not paying any particular attention to the gun-hung cowboy behind them, apparently dozing in a chair balanced on its two back legs against the wall.

Not until Hensen and Walker split up did Bern rise in an easy, almost lazy motion. After he'd watched the showdown bet between Walker and Maize Jackson a couple of weeks ago, he came to a decision and he made that decision clear to Farley. He was backing Jackson all the way. Now he hurried to tell Maize what he'd overheard.

Late that afternoon Maize got up a game of freezeout, playing straight-draw. Hensen wanted in, Lin, two of the stranded stage passengers, and Farley. Walker bought in, making it seven.

Jackson's half-smirk hid the cold anger inside him. What Hensen and Walker figured to have in store for him didn't outrage him so much as that they figured him to be as stupid as they were. For cripe's sake, even without Bern's warning he'd have known those two had something cooking.

First, Walker brought hard cash to the game. Now where in hell could he have gotten it but off Hensen. And Hensen wouldn't stake a flea to a dog dinner without he figured he could get the dog to bite someone for him.

His smile stretched a little thinner as Hensen took the chair to his immediate left. Jackson bet himself a fifty-cent cigar Bull would sit at his right. He won. *God, those two are subtle*. Thinking it, Jackson almost laughed aloud.

The players took a few minutes to lay out the ground-rules before setting in to earnest play. Straight draw.

Freezeout—once a player lost his initial stake, he was out. Any kind of ranking hand could open, even a pair of deuces. No checking. Even though it marked him as a weak sister, Walker insisted on the last to eliminate sandbagging. But it might cut Jackson's edge a little. Play began.

As the evening rolled on, one of the stage passengers washed out. Jackson, like most of the others, see-sawed, winning a small pot, losing a small one. He could have won and he could have won big, but that didn't fit in with his plans.

Early in the game he managed to crimp the cards so by the time the deals made a circuit of the table, every important card was marked in a way only he could read.

Figuring that Walker wouldn't start anything so long as he was winning, Jackson rigged his deal every time to let Walker take a big pot and Farley to lose it. By his manipulation of the pasteboards, Jackson had consistently worked to Walker's advantage while undercutting Farley.

As different as those two—Walker and Farley—were in appearance, they had like temperaments. Neither made a hand at poker—gloaters when winning, grousers when losing. Their personalities worked against each other as one's stack grew and the other's diminished.

Throughout the play, Jackson made a point of laying the discards between himself and Walker. On several occasions, when he made certain someone was looking, he'd twist his head quickly toward the waste pile, then look at Bull, as if expecting to catch the man with his fingers in it.

On Jackson's last deal, he worked Walker into pulling down the biggest win of the night, leaving Farley nearly as busted as the flush he tried to bluff with.

Jackson smiled to himself. He'd set the caps on the dynamite—now to light the fuse.

He received the deck from Walker and dealt the cards around. He looked at Hensen. Hensen shook his head. Unable to check and not having the cards to open, he set his cards down, saying, "I fold." Nursing his small stakes, Lin did the same.

The play moved on to Farley. "Open." He pushed his two-dollar bet to the middle of the table. The whiskey drummer on his left called.

Stifling a brief grin, Walker said, "Raise you two."

"Dealer calls." Jackson looked to Farley.

"See you and raise you five."

The drummer called. Walker saw and raised another two dollars. This time both Jackson and Farley called.

Scooping up Hansen and Lin's dead hands, Jackson laid them between himself and Walker.

"What'll it be?" he said to Farley.

Farley, holding two queens, kept back an ace kicker. "Gimme two."

As Jackson raked in Farley's discards, he let the bottom one—the king of hearts—flash to the drummer.

The dummer said, "I'll take three."

Bull held two pairs—kings and sevens. "I'll take one."

He dropped his discards on the pile between him and Jackson. Jackson frowned, certain that drummer caught his look.

"Dealer takes three. You bet," he said to Farley.

Jackson dealt him another queen, so now the little outlaw held three queens, the ace kicker, and a trey. With jacks and fours and an ace, the drummer stayed in.

On Bull's draw, Jackson passed him Farley's discarded king of hearts. So now Walker had a full house, kings over sevens. "See you and raise you ten."

Jackson folded. Farley and the drummer stayed in, calling. Farley didn't have enough money to do more, and the drummer, suspicions aroused, had no desire to get in too deep.

"What've you got?" the drummer asked.

Walker turned his hand over. "Kings over sevens."

Almost in unison, Farley and the drummer scraped their chairs back and jumped to their feet.

"How the hell did you get that king of hearts?" the drummer demanded.

"Jackson dealt it to me on my draw," Walker frowned, not understanding what was going on.

"The hell he did!" Farley stood by the table, his gunhand swinging free. "I discarded that king of hearts!"

"That's right! I saw it when Jackson raked in his discards!" the drummer backed up Farley.

"You damn crook," Farley shouted, "no wonder you been cleaning up all night!"

"Why you son-of-a-bitch—" Walker pushed away from the table.

There was a sudden explosion of flame and gunsmoke, the air ringing with shouts and curses and toppling chairs. An instantaneous hush followed. Everything had happened so fast, no one could say for certain who drew first or who even got into the action. But in such close quarters the toll was heavy.

Bandy, who'd been watching the game over Lin's shoulder took a bad one through the chest and the whiskey drummer was also seriously wounded. Even Hensen got nicked inside his upper arm, a handspan from his heart. But Walker cashed in his chips—permanently.

As the haze lifted, Hensen, stunned by the suddenness of it all thought he saw Jackson slipping his gun back into leather. He held his own gun still in his hand—never had a chance to get off a shot.

He looked at Jackson again. The gunman ever so slightly tipped his head, the barest kind of smile lifting the corners of his lips, but never reaching the chipped blue ice of his eyes.

XXII

The single wire between Pipe Spring and Salt Lake City stayed in operation and provided their one line with the outside world.

The storm, already close to four weeks old, was the worst in anyone's memory. Cattle were dying by the tens of thousands across the plains and through the mountain ranges. Homesteaders in their shacks, outriders, stranded travelers cut off from everything and everybody froze to death.

Where people congregated, violence abounded. The enforced idleness, worry over loved ones or livestock, crowding, shortages of supplies shortened tempers and spiced reactions. Pipe Spring experienced it and on a smaller scale, so did the four imprisoned at 3-H.

Christmas day and the following week proved a living hell for Race. The silent tension between him and Sage dragged at him like quicksand. He spent as much time outside as possible, but there was only so much wood to cut, so many animals to feed—and it was so damned cold outside, well below zero the whole time.

When he wasn't taking meals with the others, Race secluded himself in the bunkroom with stacks of books borrowed from Libby. But the spirit had gone out of him. The confinement started to wear on his nerves, too reminiscent of Laramie. When he'd been there in the pen, he'd seen a number of men succumb to the "prison shakes," that peculiar nervousness that weakens a man, breaks his spirit and robs him of all dignity.

A couple of times Race had teetered on that brink. He recognized the symptoms and feared heading that direction now. Something had to break—the weather, the tension between him and Sage, or Race himself.

Then it came—the chinook—warm, snow-melting winds. Within three days, the land had turned into a sea of mud. Welcome as the chinook had been, it brought hours of unrelenting labor with it. He buried Stubbs and the other man he'd found. He stayed hours in the saddle, changing horses often, trying to locate the cattle, tallying losses.

But the backbreaking work provided the physical release Race needed, pulling him outside himself, drawing him back to some degree of normalcy. Another week locked in that house—Race hated to think about it.

Sage hadn't fared much better and one day she dumfounded Libby by announcing, "I've decided to marry Maize."

The coffee cup clattered from Libby's hands, but she let it lie broken on the floor as she stared at Sage.

"Whatever are you talking about? You don't mean it!"

"Of course I do. Why wouldn't I?"

"You hardly know him!"

"I've known him longer than you knew Bull when you married him."

"Do you love Jackson?"

Sage answered with a question of her own, "Did you love Bull when you married him?"

Libby's shoulders drooped. "No. I married him to use him."

Sage looked at her quickly, saw that her cousin was not being sarcastic. She really meant it.

"Libby, you're serious aren't you?"

"You're damn right I am." Sage had never heard Libby swear before and that compounded her shock.

"Libby, I don't think I know you."

"You don't. And you know Maize Jackson even less. What's brought this all about?"

"He's asked me several times and I've just come to a decision."

130

"That damn Jackson," Libby whispered under her breath. "Listen Sage, that night we took the kettle of broth down to Race, Maize propositioned me. It was because of him I married Bull in the first place. Ever since we found your parents dead, Maize has hounded me constantly to marry him. When we got here and Bull showed interest in me, I encouraged him, hoping to slow Maize down a little. That didn't work.

"My first husband was the only man I ever loved. I didn't want to get married again, but Jackson forced my hand. When Bull admitted to me he'd been—well, emasculated by a shell he'd taken during the war, I made my mind up. I thought I could marry him and still be faithful to my first husband's memory, and most important of all put a buffer between Jackson and me. I get sick and ashamed every time I think of what I've done. It's not been fair to Bull or to myself and it hasn't stopped Jackson one bit.

"Now you tell me you want to marry Jackson. He's intriguing, I admit, but why now? It's got something to do with Race, hasn't it? I don't know what went on between you two, but it's not been easy living with either one of you. He's become a hermit and you walk around with a face long enough to trip over.

"But marrying Jackson isn't the answer. Knowing that he's been after me, even after I married Bull, doesn't that tell you something about the man?"

"Libby, I like you a lot, but I don't know that Maize has been after you—only that you tell me he has. You admit you find him intriguing. Are you sure that deep down you just don't want Jackson flapping around footloose and fancy free for your own reasons?"

Libby stiffened, then suddenly her hand flashed out and caught Sage across the face. Tears flooding her eyes, Sage lifted a hand to her stinging cheek, then turned and fled to the privacy of her room.

At once startled and regretful at what she'd done, Libby reached out a hand in contrition, but the younger woman never saw it. Sage had no mother, no other woman to turn to. Libby had been like a sister to her. The slap cut like no words could.

131

With sadness Sage remembered how she had slapped Race's face. Now she sensed some of the hurt and humiliation he must have felt. With a moan, Sage stretched full out across her bed and cried.

At the first opportunity that presented itself after that, Libby cornered Race.

"Race, you've got to talk to Sage."

"Me? What about?"

"She intends to marry Maize Jackson."

Hiding the sting of disappointment, he said, "What's that got to do with me?"

"Everything. From what she's told me, he's been after her for months. But she never gave his proposals serious consideration until whatever happened between you two the other day."

"Nothing happened between us the other day. I broke my word to you and got out of line. She put me in my place. It's simple as that."

"But it isn't. Race don't be blind. She's bucked you from the start because she's attracted to you in a way she never has been by any other man. You just don't understand women."

Race held back a short bitter laugh. That was sure as hell true. Twice he'd made a fool of himself over a woman—first with Jen, then the other night with Sage. He wouldn't make that kind of mistake again. There was only one kind of woman for a man like him—one who'd sell him what he needed any Saturday night.

He said, "Libby, she can do anything she damn well pleases. It's none of my business. Let's just leave it at that. Besides, she could probably do worse. At least Jackson's got a clean backtrail."

"Does he? Do any of us know that? Let me tell you some things about friend Jackson . . ." Libby filled Race in on all that she had told Sage and more.

Race understood why Libby hadn't confided any of this with her husband. With Bull's temper, he'd have called Jackson on it and gotten himself killed.

132

"Race, I believe Jackson's out to get this outfit any way he can. Through marriage or murder and I suspect he already has. But that's something I can't back up. It's just a feeling."

Frowning he said, "Then why don't you tell Sage. She'd listen to you a hell of a lot quicker than she would me."

Libby's shoulders fell in a small gesture of defeat. "I tried. But I went at it all wrong. We quarreled and I slapped her face." Race's face hardened at that. Libby lifted her hands, "I know. Don't say it. The thing is I did do it and if I say anything else to her now, I might just throw her into Jackson's arms."

"Hensen ought to be getting back any time now. Talk to him."

"No one talks to Josh about anything. How about you? When he returns will you stay on?"

"Not likely."

"After all the work you've done, he's bound to offer you a job now."

He shook his head. "Wouldn't make any difference if he did."

"Why?"

"For God's sake, Libby." he wondered if she had any idea of the hell he endured these days, being in the house with Sage day in and day out, thinking about her, holding himself back.

"Soon as he gets back, I'm fogging out of here."

XXIII

The sixth day of the chinook Race dragged in to find the extra horses in the corral. Hensen and his crew were back. So was someone else. There was one horse he didn't recognize as having been in the cavvy that first day he came. Climbing to the top rail of the daypen, he opened a loop and made his cast. The horse ducked at the rope's whir, but the catch fell true. Once the horse felt the rope on its neck, it settled down and came at Race's tug.

A swift check—no brand. Might mean something or not. Slipping thong from hammer, Race loosened his gun in its holster before heading for the house.

As he reached the steps he heard, "*Raza, aqui*, here!" Jésus hissed to him from the meat storage room under the porch.

His one foot already on the first step, Race had to lean backwards to see where Jésus was calling from. He stepped back down to join the old man. Jésus stood inside the room, his head just clearing the five-and-a-half-foot ceiling of the cell-like cubicle. Instead of joining the old man inside, Race hunkered down by the opening, his shoulder against the doorframe.

"What's up?"

"*Señor* Hensen is back."

He nodded, "Saw the horses."

But he is different. So much has happened. First, let me tell you. *Señor* Walker is dead—shot to death."

"Walker? How'd it happen?"

Knowing how garbled stories get in their re-telling, Jésus took his time, relaying as faithfully as possible the version he had heard.

When he finished, Race said, "Hard for me to picture Walker neat-handed enough to palm a card. How's Libby taking it?"

"Not well, *amigo. Señorita* Hensen is with her now. She is packing to leave."

"Who, Miz Walker?"

Jésus nodded. That didn't make sense to Race. From what Libby had told him, he knew she was probably feeling a lot of guilt along about now. But that about leaving—why? All she had in the world now was right here. He voiced his thoughts to the old man.

"She no longer has a share in the ranch, *Raza*. That devil Jackson won it from *Señor* Walker two weeks before. He has the paper."

"A bet like that's no good—it's Libby's property, not Bull's to begin with."

Jésus lifted his thin shoulders. "You know the *Señora*. She will honor her husband's debts."

"But I can't believe Jackson would be bastard enough to hold her to it!"

"That *chulo!*" Jésus spat on the ground. "There is nothing beyond him. But his days are numbered, my friend." As he spoke, he drew a gleaming *poignard* from the leather sheath behind his neck and released it suddenly. The razor-honed blade penetrated the doorframe like a hot knife into butter. As he tugged the knife out of the woodwork, he repeated, "His days are numbered."

Race chewed a while on what Jésus told him before asking, "Know whose hoss that dun is?"

"It must be the new man's, Bern. Bandy was also shot in that affair. Lin has stayed on with him at Pipe Spring. With three men short, *Señor* Hensen hired this Bern. But *Raza*—I think he is Jackson's man."

"Damn!" Ever since the chinook began, Race had primed himself to take off as soon as Hensen returned. But how could he leave now? What Jésus just told him, taken in combination with what Libby had confided, Race was convinced that Jackson really was after the outfit. He didn't give a damn about Hensen. Hell, Hensen wasn't on the square himself, making Race that under-the-table offer

135

that night down at the barn. But the women were sure enough between a rock and a hard place. And Sage and Libby had both been damn good to him. He brushed his hand against his coat, feeling the bulk of Sage's small Bible inside. Kindnesses had been too few in his life to overlook all they had done for him this past month.

Wasn't Sage's fault he'd made a jack-ass of himself the other night. Besides there was the one thing he hadn't admitted to anybody but couldn't deny to himself—he loved her and nothing that happened changed his feelings about that. Hell you couldn't push feelings as strong as that aside like dusk does the end of the day.

"Where's Miz Walker now?"

"Upstairs—in her room, I think."

"Keep your eyes and ears open, *Tío*. We'll make some more *habla* later."

"*A buen seguro.*"

Race walked right through the house, nodding to Hensen, but not stopping to talk. He went to the foot of the stairs and called up to Libby.

"Miz Walker, can I come up?"

A woman's voice told him to come ahead, but he couldn't tell whether it was Libby's or Sage's. At the top of the steps he paused. He'd never been in this part of the house before and he didn't know which room was Libby's. Voices drifted to him from the far end of the hall.

" . . . but there's no reason to leave. Anything I have is yours, Libby. Are you still angry with me? Is that why . . ."

"No. I'm not angry and I never really was. You just happened to cut closer to the truth than I was willing to admit. It hurt and I wanted to hurt back. But things being what they are—with Jackson here, knowing your feelings about him, what I know about him—it'd just be an impossible situation. Come on now, chin up. I'll keep in touch."

"Please. Don't go. I can't help feeling responsible."

"Don't. There's no reason for you to."

Race tapped lightly at the wide-opened door. "Miz Walker, can I talk to you . . ." he looked at Sage, then

136

added, " . . . alone?"

"I'll go," Sage said. She smiled at Libby without looking at Race. Glancing back as she stepped through the doorway, she saw Libby, tears streaming down her face, take a step toward Race. Awkwardly, he extended his arms to comfort her and she came into them.

With an inexplicable sense of loss, Sage closed the door behind her.

Race spent the next half hour in earnest conversation with Libby before finally persuading her to stay, at least for a while. The argument that won in the end was that Sage needed her.

In turn he assured her, "I'll go see Hensen now, see if he'll let me stay on. I might have to go along with him on some things that won't set right on the top of it. Just remember whose side I'm on."

He hadn't told Libby about the offer Hensen made that night, and for Sage's sake he wouldn't. All he could do was hope Libby would take the hint and trust him come hell or high water.

When Race came downstairs, he saw Hensen by the fireplace. A tall well-built man lounged in the archway between the kitchen and the big room, one hand braced against the upward curve. Black curls tumbled over a well-formed forehead. Must be the new man Bern.

Too damn pretty, Race grunted to himself, at the same time acknowledging the stab of jealousy for what it was. Bern wasn't standing alone, but enjoying an animated talk with Sage. And although she was coated, belted, and holding the milk bucket, she didn't seem the least uncomfortable.

When she glanced in Race's direction, he nodded, but she turned her head away, stepped around Bern through the kitchen to the outside.

The muscles along his jaw showed a slight tightening, but he forced himself to relax as he approached Hensen. Jackson was there with the boss.

Race asked Hensen, "Got a minute?"

Hensen looked to Jackson before nodding. Jésus was right—Hensen was different. It took a minute for Race to pinpoint it, but there it was. *Hensen was afraid*—afraid of Jackson.

"Guess Miz Walker or Miss Hensen filled you in on what's been going on around here."

"Yeah. So what do you want, a medal?" In talking to him, some of the man's old arrogance returned.

"No," Race said. "No medal. Just hoped you might of changed your mind about taking me on. If you haven't, I figured to be needing some travel money. Thought you might buy my saddle. You made me an offer for it before."

Hensen snorted, almost denying such a thing when the significance of Race's words banged home. The drifter wanted in.

"Well, I am running a little shorthanded right now. And from what the women told me, you probably saved most of my cattle. Let me get my coat. We'll walk down to the barn and look at it then I'll decide which is worth more to me—you or your saddle."

The moment they entered the darkened barn, Hensen pulled his gun and rammed the muzzle into Race's spine.

"What the hell?"

"Easy." Hensen pulled the doors shut. "Let's step a little further back here in case friend Jackson followed."

"If you're worried about him, then why the hell have you got your gun stuck in my back!"

"Just want to be sure I read your sign right. Talk."

"You read it right and you damn well know it. I caught onto your game soon as I saw that big bunch gathered all nice and neat. You're aiming to rustle off your own stock and squeeze the women out that way."

"It didn't start that way, but that's the plan now."

"All right. So now you've got Jackson muscling in. He ain't a woman and he don't squeeze. He's already got Libby's share and he'll marry Sage to get hers, if she'll let him. If you want to hang onto this place, you're going to need a gun you can trust covering your flank."

"You?"

"Me."

"A gun I can trust." Hensen rubbed his forehead. "You

138

been hanging around the women five, six weeks. Just now you had a long palaver with Libby in her bedroom. How do I know you ain't just trying to beat Jackson at his own game?''

The bitterness in Race's laugh wasn't altogether feigned. "I already tried my hand at that. Your little sister chewed me up and spit out the pieces. Didn't have any better luck with Libby—that's why I'm hitting you now. Besides, what'd a drifter like me want with an outfit and a woman to tie him down? I'm in this for whatever cash I can get out of it—which means a hundred a month not the seventy-five you offered me a month ago.''

"You're crazy.''

"Okay. Maybe Jackson'll hire me. I'll go talk to him.''

"All right, goddammit. Just remember when it comes down to the wire, don't go soft on me if the women get in the way.

Race laughed shortly. "Stories of Texas chivalry are highly exaggerated. I told you—that's the least of your worries. I got a long rope, a short iron, and a brace of guns. Say the word and I'm your man, bought and paid for. Name my first job.''

Hensen nodded. "Let's ride out. I can show you better than tell you.''

As they led their mounts out, Race caught a flash of movement at the back stall. He put a detaining hand on Hensen's arm and whispered, "Wait a minute.''

Dropping reins, Race pulled his gun and walked soundlessly to the back of the barn. At the next to the last stall, he took a quick leap and cocking his gun at the same time jumped inside the nearest corner of the open stall.

Pushing the old milch cow's rump with his free hand, Race found Sage crouched in the opposite corner, pale bars of light filtering through on her face. He swore under his breath, remembering her up to the house, her coat on, the milk bucket in her hand. She'd come down to milk the cow.

His lips thinned. Just the damn fact that she was trying to hide told him she'd heard every damn word between him and Hensen. He sighed. Nothing for it now.

They just stared at each other a long moment. Sage's face showed no fear, but what it did show sent a spike of ice through Race's heart.

Swearing to himself he turned suddenly, sheathed his gun, and rejoined Hensen. "Nothing there but the old milch cow. Let's get cracking."

Unobserved from the loft another set of eyes and ears absorbed all that had taken place. But whatever his reaction was, the breed Paiute's stolid face revealed none of it.

XXIV

Race read the note again.

> *R.*
>
> *Any idea what's going on? Sage is packing—wants to leave first thing in the morning and for me to go with her. One good thing—it means she's changed her mind about marrying Jackson, thank God!*
>
> *Overheard something else. Must talk with you. Tomorrow before dawn, under the porch?*
>
> *L.*

Crumbling the note into a ball, he threw it into the potbellied stove. If he'd only known Libby slipped a note into the book she gave him at supper—here, he'd gone and left the book on his bunk until now. Even if someone else did read it, he guessed no real harm would come of it.

Of course, it had to be the talk he'd had with Hensen that Sage overheard that lit the fire under her. Race tried to recall in detail everything that was said. Along with the rest, she must have heard them discussing Jackson's trying to marry into the ranch. Poor kid probably figured there wasn't a damn man in the world worth trusting.

But as for her and Libby leaving, the more Race thought about it, the better he liked the idea. He didn't believe either of the women was in physical danger, but the longer Sage hung around here, the more deeply she was bound to be hurt.

When he met with Libby in the morning, he'd backtrack on his earlier arguments and encourage her to leave with Sage. Maybe he'd tag along until they safely got wherever they were going, then he'd cut his picket pin and drift.

Jackson hit his bunk that night in an unusual state of agitation. He'd told Hensen he'd break the news to Libby about Bull, thinking the grieving widow would come to him for comfort. When she didn't react like she was supposed to, he tried to use his share of the ranch as a lever.

She told him, "You've got my share of the ranch. It's what you wanted, now keep it. But if I ever find out you've worked the same kind of deal with Sage, so help me, I'll come after you with a gun myself."

Then that note she slipped to the drifter tonight. Intercepting it and passing it on was no problem with his peculiar talents. So Sage had planned on marrying him! What made her change her mind? Libby, probably. And what was it Libby overheard? One of his talks with Bern or with the Paiute? As long as she was around, he'd have to be more careful—a hell of a lot more careful.

Rather than bet blind, Maize went to see Sage, to sound her out. She turned out as unresponsive as Libby. When he persisted, she told him, "Maize, I don't know how this will affect your concern for me but I think you should know I signed my share of the ranch back to Josh not fifteen minutes ago. Until today I had no idea how much this ranch meant to him. Now that I do, I'd rather he have it. The only reason I came here in the first place was because he's all the family I have. I hoped to be some help to him."

What Sage told Jackson threw him offstride. At the moment all he could think was he'd drawn another bust hand. Almost too late he realized he should bluff it through. After all, if anything happened to Hensen—and he'd see that it would—she'd be his only heir.

"For your sake, I'm sorry you did that, Sage. But if you think that was the right thing to do, why then I'm glad you did it. What are your plans now?"

"Beyond leaving, I don't have any. Maybe I'll go back to the mission school. They always need teachers."

"Well, I'll escort you there. Don't worry."

"We'll see . . . and thanks, Maize—you just put the lie to something I heard." She put her hand on his.

So that part of it worked out all right—until the next time Libby would throw a wrench in the works. That woman was getting to be a real problem.

And where the hell did that drifter fit in? Jackson's eyes clouded as he rolled and lit a cigarette in the darkness. Moonlight silhouetted Race's bunk across the way.

He and Libby must have had something going between them all the time Walker was away. That was sure some long parlay they'd had up in her bedroom this afternoon. Was Libby intending to sic the drifter on him? Jackson laughed under his breath. It'd take better than the two of them together to beat him at his own game.

He'd cut them out of the picture. Jackson smiled, appreciating the irony of it—Libby herself had given him the means to do it.

Race shifted restlessly. Already pale pink strands threaded the eastern sky, but Libby still hadn't showed. It finally dawned on him she might be inside the storeroom waiting for him. She certainly wouldn't have the fear of entering that cell-like chamber that he did.

He shoved the door open and bent low to peer inside.

"Miz Walker? Libby?" Stooping, he entered, kicked something on the floor, nearly tripping over it. Race fumbled with a lit match.

"Aw, God, no . . ."

Libby lay on the dirt floor, her face bloodied and bruised, her skirt up around her waist, her undergarments torn as if an animal had been at her. He knelt beside her and gently pulled down the skirt to cover her exposed thighs and legs.

Sickness and a roiling fury swelled up in him, but he just stayed there in confused helplessness for uncounted minutes, blaming himself—first for talking her into staying, then for not getting to that note before someone else apparently did.

A piercing scream jerked him back to life. Hitching around, he saw Sage outside the opening, limned by the morning's first light. At first she seemed paralyzed. But the first step he took toward her galvanized her into action. He barely made it through the opening before she was on him, wild as a bronc hauling hell out of a shuck, using feet, nails, and fists.

Race stuck both arms out, trying to keep distance between them until she calmed down enough for him to talk to her. Afraid of hurting her, he back-stepped a pace. Out of nowhere, lightning pain forked through his skull, followed by an explosion of garish color. Dimly he clung to consciousness, spiralling into deeper blackness with each vicious chop that raked his head. As he fell, he saw Jackson slashing his gun wildly, buffaloing him with the sharpened front sight of his revolver. Even after Race lay unconscious, the gunman continued to flail at his unprotected head.

Race lay face down in the mud, Jackson over him. As Maize brought his arm back again, Sage grabbed it, screaming, "Stop it! You'll kill him!"

Jésus materialized out of nowhere, lending his strength to Sage's. "Get back, you damn greaser!" Jackson turned on him, swiping at his head and opening the old man's cheek with the gunsight.

"Stop it Maize! Have you gone crazy!"

Jackson pulled up short, swearing. *All this damn interference*! Panting he told Sage, "Sorry I lost my head when I saw that bum mauling you, especially after what he did to Libby."

Something about Jackson's sudden appearance, his attack, even his words jarred Sage. But she was too concerned about Libby to stop and analyze it. "Let's tend to Libby."

Jackson grabbed her by the wrist. "There's nothing we can do for her. She's dead. God, I can't understand why they ever let trash like that out of jail." He booted Race's limp body.

Everything had happened so fast! Sage hadn't time to sort out one impression from the other. The fact that Libby was dead hadn't fully registered yet and as Hensen came roaring out of the house, Sage was in near shock.

"Now what the hell's going on!"

"Your jailbird friend just murdered Libby. I came out in time to catch him manhandling Sage, too! Tell him!"

144

Now that Sage had a chance to think about it, she realized Race hadn't touched her. She shook her head as if to clear it.

"No," she said. "I came down to get some bacon for breakfast. I saw Libby . . . when I saw her like that . . . and Race beside her . . I guess I got a little hysterical. But no, he didn't lift a hand to me."

Jackson breathed an oath. He'd have to watch it—Sage Hensen was one person he couldn't manipulate worth a damn. Like any experienced card sharp, Jackson fell back on an old reliable trick of the trade—diverting attention from himself. "Well, you can't say Walker didn't warn us about men like this. Take a look at Libby. Look what that damn jailbird did to her!"

The voices came and faded. On the ground Race groped toward consciousness, his fingers digging into the mud as if he could literally pull himself out of his numbed stupor.

Hensen saw Jésus then. "And what the hell happened to you?"

The old man nodded his head toward Jackson. "He was trying to kill *Raza*."

"You're damn right I was." Just as Race struggled to his one knee, Jackson turned on him, kicking out viciously and catching the cowboy along the side of his head. Race dropped soddenly, blood streaming from his mouth, nose, and ears.

Jésus scrambled to Race's side, lifted his head from the mud and cradled it in his arms. Looking up at Jackson, he hissed, "*Bastardo!*"

Jackson looked down at the slight old man, his lips slowly curling into that quirky half-smile. The expression froze on his face as the Paiute came up behind Hensen. The Indian breed was staring at him and for no reason at all, Jackson thought of the greaser's threat and a cold black chill filled him.

XXV

The fetor of dried blood and sour earth stung Race's nostrils. Jerking his head away from the rancid smells set off a series of erratic explosions in his skull. With a groan, he froze, waiting for the pain to ease.

A paste of mud and his own blood caked and dried on his face, sealing his eyes shut. Working gingerly, he fingered them clean, flecks gritting under his eyelids.

Slowly he rolled to one side. Even that motion churned up a new spike of pain and nausea. Blinking to clear his eyes, he made out a vague gray blot against the blackness. He closed his eyes again, trying to draw them in focus. When he opened them, what he saw clinched his stomach into strangling knots.

The emaciated sickle of moon grudgingly shed enough light to outline the small barred window at the top of the door.

A series of jolting memories—unwashed bodies in cramped cells, stinking slop jars and rancid food, seam squirrels crawling over his clothes, pallet and in the hairy parts of his body, club-wielding screws, all too willing and ready to use them—unreasoning panic shot through Race.

He vaulted to his feet, cracking his head and shoulders against the low ceiling. Oblivious to the pain hatcheting through his skull, he reached for the strap iron bars and tore at them with his hands.

The sharp edges cut his hands into a raw and bloody mess. But he clung to them until spasms of wild trembling geysered up and through him. His body began to shake uncontrollably.

Somehow that potent threat of going into the "prison shakes" slammed reason back into him.

Oh, God, don't let my nerve quit me now.

Forcing his fingers to uncurl, Race let go the flat-iron

bars and sank to the ground, fighting for control of himself.

This isn't Laramie, dammit, get hold of yourself.

Sharp pain throbbed rhythmically inside his head, but he forced himself to look at his surroundings. He was in the meat storage room under the porch, the room where he had found Libby. The memory brought a surge of grief, but he had himself cinched up tight now.

A single thought stood out clearly—whoever ravaged Libby was still ranging free and wide and would as long as everyone else thought Race did it. And where the hell did that leave Sage?"

Right off the top he could think of two more likely prospects than himself—Farley and Jackson. He knew Farley'd been up for murdering a woman. And he knew Libby feared and distrusted Jackson. Even Hensen was a possibility. Bad as the big augur wanted to hold this outfit for himself, maybe he had something like this in mind when he took Race on.

Setting on his spurs wouldn't get the horse roweled, but under the circumstances, there wasn't much more he could do than think—and even that hurt like hell.

Race woke up shivering on the dirt floor some hours past midnight. A new chill weighted the air, one that hadn't been there since the chinook began. They might be in for some new weather.

He rose slowly, careful not to jar his battered head or bump it on the low ceiling. From what he could see through the strap-iron window, Hensen hadn't set a guard on him. Probably figured him for half-dead. At that they weren't far off. Maybe they figured if they just let him lie there long enough, he'd cash in his chips and save them the bother of doing the job.

Swearing under his breath, Race searched the little storeroom for something to pry, dig, or smash his way out of there. He scoured the floor, the walls, even the short ceiling, but the damn sides of beef hanging around three walls hampered him.

Suddenly he snapped his fingers. Jackson must've scrambled my brains worse than I figured, he muttered under his breath. Breathing a mild oath, he lifted down

147

one of the sides of beef and withdrew the meathook. The elongated iron "S," blunt on one end, sharply pointed at the other gave him a tool to work with—or a weapon.

Right now it would make a dandy pry. Probably make a hell of a racket against the bars, but no help for that.

He stepped soundlessly to the metal lattice and with painstaking care to keep the skreak of metal against metal to a minimum, he worked the pointed end under the bottom of one of the metal laths and levered. He freed all the straps across the bottom, then worked up each side until the rusty grating hung only by the top. He swung it out like a hinge, applying slow steady pressure.

The opening was small, less than a foot square, but it gave Race access to the swing hasp outside. He reached through and swore.

Someone had replaced the peg in the staple with a padlock. From the feel of the lock, it might be a "ward" lock. If it were, even the improved model with tumblers, it shouldn't be too hard to work. A wry smile quirked his lips. Good to know his early training was coming in handy for something. Until he'd tied up with Ruby Evans, there hadn't been a storage shed in any town safe from his talented fingers.

He cast around in the dark until he came up with a length of stiff wire. A single bend and a little jiggling should do it.

That's all it would have taken, except for two things—he had to work one-handed and blind. With his face on one side of the door, his left arm through the opening clear up to the shoulder, he had to probe awkwardly, the lock swinging on its clasp with every move he made.

There was no way he could stabilize the lock as he worked. It would just take time and patience. He had the patience, but what about the time?

A soft sigh of relief escaped as he felt the clasp finally swing free of the barrel of the lock. Lifting off the padlock, he eased the door open. Belly down, he snaked through the opening. A voice, menacing in its quietness, reached out like a disembodied spirit to embrace him.

"Took you long enough. Beginning to wonder if you

were ever gonna make it." The voice didn't drown out the click of a gun going on cock.

Jackson. Race expected it. His mind hadn't been idle while he'd been locked up. He knew Jackson had to kill him and why he'd waited until now.

Not answering, Race shifted direction and rose to a crouch, gripping the meathook by its lighter end, ready to throw it at the next breath of movement from Jackson.

Then it came—Jackson's whisper, taunting, trying to trip Race into exposing his position while he shifted locations himself as he talked.

"Took you long enough, jailbird—forty-three minutes by my—"

Jackson could afford to wait, but Race couldn't. He heaved the iron at the sound of Jackson's voice, following close on it with a leap, arms widespread. The hook missed Jackson, but Race didn't. He slammed Jackson back into the mud and heard the man's gun slosh away.

Both were quick for their size, but with Race's bad leg, Maize had the edge. He pushed to his feet bringing one knee up hard against Race's chest. Unable to get solid purchase in the thaw-softened earth, Maize fell forward onto Race. Race wrapped his arms around the gunman. Jackson brought his knee against him again, barely missing Race's groin. Race let go, rolling free.

Both lunged to their feet, two tall animal-mad shadows coming at each other whip and spur—fighting without science, swinging savagely, wanting only to smash and destroy.

Race drove a left solidly to the point of Jackson's jaw, driving him to his knees. While down, the gunman wrapped his arms around Race's legs and pulled his feet out from under him.

Again they lurched to their feet, the heavy blue clay dragging at them, slowing them down. As he rose, Jackson whipped loose his belt, fisting the brass buckle, its sharp metal tongue erected between the grooves of his fingers. When Race closed with him, Jackson slashed at his eyes, trying to gouge them out with the sharp prong.

An old hand at gutter-fighting himself, Race threw one

149

arm up to protect his face, feinted with the other. As he pulled Jackson off guard, he stomped down viciously on the gunman's instep then brought the same leg up, folded, into Maize's groin.

Bent over and gasping for breath, Jackson clinched, pinning Race's upper arms. Race drove his thumbs under the gunman's jaw then flung his arms wide, breaking Jackson's hold.

Sheer nerve and roiling hate carried Race this far, but he was hurting. His battered head was vulnerable, and worst of all, Jackson knew it.

Without any finesse, Jackson went to work on Race's head, thundering lefts and rights, getting past Race's guard and landing solidly.

Race grabbed Jackson, pressing his head hard against the other's, playing for time to clear his head. Unable to break the hold of Race's work-hardened arms, Jackson wrapped his right leg behind Race's left and dragged his razor-sharp rowel down the back of the cowboy's leg. Raking again, at the downstroke he hooked his spur behind Race's bootheel and jerked forward.

Race jarred heavily to the ground. By pure instinct he rolled in time to avoid Jackson's grinding bootheel in his face. Before Race could roll again, Jackson, with his superior weight advantage, jumped astride. He dug both fists into the cowboy's hair, lifted then slammed . . .lifted, then slammed. Each concussion sent ungodly spasms of pain spidering through Race's head.

Fighting to keep conscious, Race worked his arms out from under Jackson, groping frantically for the gunman's throat. His strength lay in his hands and he used them now. Like some violent Mexican standoff, the outcome would depend on who could outlast who.

Another savage slam dimmed Race's vision. With everything turning black, his fingers still clung to Jackson's throat like a sprung bear trap.

From a far-off distance he heard a voice—insistent, urgent.

"Por Dios! Raza! Poir Dios!"

Race stared blankly at Jésus while the old man pried him

150

and Jackson apart. Jackson rolled limply into the mud alongside the cowboy. In a daze, Race dragged to his feet.

The old man's wiry hands pulled at him. "*Aprisa!* Hurry, *amigo*, before he wakes up!"

With keen disappointment, he stared at Jésus. He'd hoped Jackson was dead. He wanted to finish it, but as he tried to get his rubbery legs moving under him, a suffocating sickness filled him. Folding at the middle, Race began to retch dryly.

"*Por Dios, Raza.* Before the others come . . . over here, your horse. I have him saddled. *Raza*, do you understand?"

Race looked at the old man glassy-eyed. "Got to kill that son-of-a-bitch."

Jésus shook his head. Race was simply out on his feet. Supporting the cowboy as best he could, he led Race to the waiting buckskin.

"You must leave. Do you understand?"

"Jackson—"

"No."

"—he killed Libby."

"The others would shoot you down before you could say a word! *Raza, por Dios*, go now before Jackson wakes up. He is already stirring!"

Race was sick and his head pounded and he couldn't think. He let Jésus foot him up into the saddle. Swallowing hard against his nausea, he hung sickly over the pommel.

"Can you ride, *amigo*?"

Race nodded, the motion sending a wave of blackness over him. Vaguely he watched while Jésus flipped out his *cuchillo*. The Mexican slit open the seam between the leg and lining of Race's boot and inserted the knife there.

"Hensen! Hensen! He's getting away!" On his feet and staggering toward them, Jackson sounded the alarm.

Quickly, Jésus knotted the reins, threw them over the saddlehorn and slapped the rump of the mare. At his wild yell, Race's buckskin lunged wildly forward, carrying her slack burden into the promised protection of the night.

Straightening his thin shoulders, Jésus turned to face Jackson.

XXVI

Like a kicked-over ant hill the 3-H crew spilled out of the house, Sage close behind. Lanterns raised, they formed a semi-circle around the bitterly swearing Maize Jackson.

Jésus' shriveled body twitched along the ground. Already dead, reflex action kept him moving as diminishing amounts of blood spurted from his slit jugular.

"That jailbird, goddamn him! Came out to check on him—just had a damn feeling—he jumped me in the dark. Caught me off guard, beat me into the ground—nearly strangled me to death before I even knew what was happening." Massaging his throat, Maize spoke in a hoarse, crackly voice.

"Jésus called . . . I remember that . . . but then things kind of blacked out for a moment or two. When I got my senses back, I saw Evans going after him. I yelled, but it was too damn late. He'd already grabbed the Mex's knife and used it on him. Worst of it is, it's all my fault!"

Hensen threw him a sharp look. "What do you mean?"

"I knew about him. Farley told me at Pipe Spring. Dammit, don't look at me that way. That's exactly why I didn't talk up when I should have. I knew you'd take it wrong. But hell, Hensen, I saw you making palaver with that damn rustler yourself. Anyway, according to Farley, he shared a cell up at Laramie with Evans. He lied when he told you he was in for rustling. He was in for murdering a woman. He was doing hard time, got so rough to handle, they shipped him to Nebraska. He broke out of there not more'n a year ago." Glibly, Jackson attributed Farley's prison record to Race.

"I'd have told you, but so far as I knew, he dusted out of here a month ago. When we got back and he was still here, I should've spoke up. But hell, you were down on me."

Jackson's words as much as Jésus' contorted body left Sage numb. Until this very minute, she deep-down hoped that Race really was innocent of Libby's brutal murder.

Heedless of the puddling blood, she dropped to her knees alongside Jésus and felt for the thong around his neck. She slid it around until the sheath was in front. Her heart sank—the sheath was empty.

Enough of what Jackson said corresponded to what Race had admitted to her that night, that she had no reason now to doubt Jackson's version.

But why? Why did he do it and why now? Maybe the answer to that lay within herself. Even now she could feel the pressure of his hungry lips. Maybe if she hadn't point-blank rejected him . . . it was just that she found herself wanting him in a way . . . she shook her head violently, trying to throw off the thought.

Two firm hands clasped her shoulders, lifted her to her feet, pulled her from her black reverie. Jackson turned her so that she faced him. A practiced and convincing liar, he met her eyes squarely.

"I know this's hard for you to take, Sage. Libby told me how you were stuck on that cowboy."

Sage opened her mouth to protest, but didn't. Whether Libby had told him or not, it was true. Even now, more than anything in the world, she wanted to believe Race didn't do this. With a sudden surge of self-disgust, she made herself face up to reality.

Race Evans was exactly what she first took him for, and worse—a liar, a jailbird, a murderer. Tiger was the right name for him, an animal preying on the helpless.

She forced herself to take another look at Jésus' body. Twisting away from Jackson, she walked slowly to the house alone, the hem of her blood-stained wrapper dragging the ground.

153

From behind her came her brother's voice talking to the men. "No. we ain't going after him. This is a working ranch and we ain't no damn posse. But that's as far as she goes. If you see the locoed bastard shoot him down like you would any lobo wolf."

Sage swore to herself, given half a chance, she'd kill Race Evans herself.

In spite of the pulsating misery each step of the mare triggered, Race held her to a steady jog. One thought dominated his state of semi-consciousness—don't let the buckskin have her head. As close as they were to the ranch, she'd make a bee-line for there if he gave her any slack.

At the woods north of the ranch, he swung east, into the dense evergreen forest. The carpet of needles softened the mare's jolting gait, thank God. Maybe they wouldn't leave as easy a trail for them to follow here as back in the mud-soft parks. Couldn't anybody trail him in the dark anyhow, could they? His thoughts were muddled and he couldn't pull them together enough to make sense.

As they jarred along, he drifted in and out of his torpor, all sense of direction lost. But he was beyond caring.

At one point he fell from his horse. The jolt of the landing set up such a godawful clamor inside his skull, he just lay there, not even trying to move. Hours later, the bitter cold roused him. Chilled with ground-stiffness in his joints, he found the sleeve of his outstretched arm frozen to the ground.

Gingerly he raised his head, worked the sleeve free and took stock. He had a concussion, no doubt of that. He'd been a bronc-snapper too many years not to recognize the symptoms. What he needed more than anything was a hole to crawl into—someplace he could sleep undisturbed around the clock. That brought up two new problems. One, where could he find such a place and two, how could he get there—the mare was gone.

As he started to rise, he discovered a third problem. A cylinder of cold steel punched against the hollow of his cheek.

"Just hold it right there, you son-of-a-bitch!"

The voice wasn't familiar, but the gun barrel against Race's face spoke the man's intent plain enough.

Race sank back onto the ground and submitted uncaring while the other ran his hands over him, searching for weapons.

"Roll over." A boot toe under his stomach accompanied the order, flipping him roughly over onto his back. Race looked straight up into the glittering eyes of Hensen's breed tracker, but he was too sick to be surprised or to give a damn.

His gun still lined on Race, the Paiute stooped, ran his hand across the front of Race's body, then inside the cowboy's boots. He found Jésus' knife and hefted it in his hand.

"Looks familiar."

Race remembered the Paiute had been at the house last night. Rather than say something that might get his friend Jésus in trouble, he kept his mouth shut.

His silence angered the breed. "It's the Mexican's, isn't it? Answer me, goddamn you!"

He back-handed Race across the face, bouncing his head against the ground. Race groaned, "Oh God . . ."

Drawing his dark eyebrows together, the breed squatted and looked more closely at Race. The drifter's condition didn't exactly go foot-in-stirrup with the way Jackson told it. How the hell did this cowboy get so battered up? He put the question to Race.

Race said, "Didn't Jackson tell you?"

"Don't play smart games with me, damn you. I asked a question. What about the Mex?"

"I don't give a damn what Jackson told you. Jésus didn't help me. I took the Mex's knife."

"Get up." The Indian herded Race toward a cabin—actually more of a shack—less than a hundred yards farther on. Race stumbled over the distance, falling a few times. The Indian made no effort to help, but he didn't push either.

Once they got inside, he directed Race to a rough bunk nailed to one wall.

"On your back and spread-eagle."

Pulling out buckskin thongs, he tied Race's wrists to the unpeeled poles at the head, then did his ankles at the other end. Across the room he built a fire and set a pan of water on it. Then he dragged the room's single chair close to the bunk and, turning it around, straddled it.

"Let's try once more. I heard Jackson's version this morning. I want to hear yours now."

Race studied the breed closely. Until today, he'd never heard the Indian speak. Instead of the grunts or guttural Pidgon-English Race expected to hear, the Indian sounded like any other cowpoke, except maybe better educated. The man obviously had something specific in mind.

"What is it to you?" Race asked.

"I've got my reasons," his voice hardened. But Race just shook his head.

"Look," the Paiute said, "I've got enough moccasin in my veins to skin your hide off inch by inch with a dull razor and never blink an eye," then he sighed, "but I've got a hunch you're the kind who'd hang and rattle. And that'd be a painful waste of time, especially for you. I'll tell you this much, it's important to me—personally—to find out just what exactly happened this morning. Level with me, Evans. You won't be sorry."

Race's head throbbed mercilessly and he probably wasn't thinking straight, but damned if he didn't believe the breed.

"I picked my way out of that storeroom. Jackson was laying for me. He killed Libby Walker and he knew I could prove it if I could get anybody to listen. He waited till I freed myself so he could claim he caught me trying to escape—which would have been the truth for a change. I slipped out of that jackpot and managed to fight Jackson to a stand-off. I woke up first and beat it the hell out of there."

"What about the Mex?"

"I told you—he had nothing to do with it."

"Then how'd you get his knife?"

Race swore under his breath, wishing he could think clearer, come up with some logical story the Indian would

156

buy. Jésus had stuck his neck out to help him and he wouldn't be the one to cut it off. Race just shook his head.

"Dammit, man! What are you hiding? The Mex is a dead man anyway."

"That a threat?"

The Paiute scrunched up his dark face. "No, that's fact. You don't live long with your throat cut. With his knife and you gone, tag—you're it."

"That's a damn lie!" Race jerked against his hobbled wrists, the rawhide giving only so far before the tension yanked him back down against the bunk. Pain lightninged through his skull. Clenching his teeth against the racking pain, he cursed Jackson bitterly in soft drawn-out accents.

Race's grief and surprise were too real to be feigned and he finally told the whole story—from the moment he found Libby until Jésus boosted him onto the buckskin.

The Paiute nodded, believing him. "That fits—but I had to be sure."

"Hensen send you here to find me?"

"No. Told you, I'm here on my own hook."

"What're you going to do now?"

"Talk to friend Jackson. If what you've told me is true, he not only killed Jésus but Libby Walker, too."

"Hell, if the whole truth ever comes out, he probably engineered Walker's killing, too."

The Paiute snorted. "Might go farther back than that—the elder Hensens didn't exactly die in their sleep you know. He's been picking them off one at a time like ticks off a hound."

"But if you say anything to Jackson, do you see where that puts Sage Hensen?" Race asked. "When he gets to thinking about it, he'll realize I need her to back up my story. Besides me, she's the only one can prove it was him not me killed Miz Walker. She hasn't realized it herself yet, but when she does she's the kind who'd throw it in his face."

"She's got her brother. He'll look after her." The Indian laid out another chunk of bait, remembering the conversation he'd overheard down at the barn between this cowboy and Hensen.

"Dammit, man! Hensen's in this up to his neck. He hired me to rook her out of her share of the ranch. I was stringing him along for my own reasons. But he don't give a single damn about Sage!"

The Paiute nodded. Race Evans was dealing square with him. He rose and stepped outside the cabin. Soon he returned with a handful of shredded aspen bark and set it in the pan of boiling water.

"Let it stew a while, then drink it. It'll help your head. Ought to be ready about the time you free yourself."

He stuck Jésus' knife into the corner pole above Race's right wrist. "Not that I don't trust you, I just don't want any interference. I've come too far along." He paused then added, "One more thing—about the girl—if my talk goes the way I plan, she'll be safe enough."

When he reached the door, he turned again to Race. "You know, I had some real doubts about you when I picked up your trail and saw you heading hell-bent for this place."

Race knitted his brows. "Where are we?"

"You really don't know, do you?"

He shook his head.

The Paiute gave Race a spare smile. "You're fifteen miles east of Hensen's. This is Kell Farley's hangout."

XXVII

Kell Farley's hangout! Race needed that like a drowning man needs a bucket of water. What a hell of a note. Nothing for it but to play the hand as the cards are dealt, 'cause he sure as hell wasn't going anywhere.

Race wondered, too, what the Paiute's stake in all this was. The man said he'd take care of Sage, but he could have meant that in any of a half dozen different ways. But damned if he didn't seem on the up and up.

As these thoughts worked rapidly through his mind, Race worked the thong around his right wrist up to the knife blade. He sawed once and the leather slit neat. In a few minutes he was freed at all corners.

Even that little exertion set his head in to throbbing meanly. He remembered the "medicine" the Indian left simmering on the iron stove. Holding his head with one hand, he straggled to the stove and smelled the concoction.

"Can't do more'n kill me," he said aloud, then sipped directly from the pot. After he tasted the stuff, he wasn't sure but what the alternative would be preferable.

Race fed and banked the fire before returning to the bunk. No sooner had he eased under the rough covers than he dropped into a dead sleep.

By morning he felt almost human. His head still ached dully, but the piercing spasms had quit. Maybe that damn stuff the Paiute brewed really worked.

It had been more than twenty-four hours since he'd last eaten and his belly was playing howdy with his backbone. Rustling around the cabin he found a slab of bacon, blue with mold, and a small crock of home-pickled cucumbers, probably stolen, knowing Kell.

Well, he'd eaten a hell of a lot worse and survived. Race scraped then sliced the bacon and set it in a pan. While the sidemeat sizzled on the stove, he stepped outside, munching on one of the pickles.

He found the buckskin in a rickety pole corral behind the shack. She was munching on food, too. A quick check showed enough feed and water to carry her a few days. All he had to do was crack the ice that formed on the trough during the night. Race eyed the sky. The weather was sure enough turning off bad again. That cut down his choices some. Actually it left him with no choice at all.

Here he had shelter and food of sorts to see him and the mare through at least until his head got better. True, chances were he'd have to take Kell Farley along with it. At best, Farley was an erratic little bugger, crazy as a flea—you never knew for sure which way he'd jump. At least if he stayed, he knew what he had to face. But out there, if he got stranded in another blizzard . . .

After he finished his meager meal, he stretched out with Sage's Bible, thinking to read until he drifted off to sleep. He opened the Book at random and began to read.

" . . . *but this one thing I do, forgetting those things which are behind, and reaching forth unto those things which are before, I' press toward the mark for the prize . . .*"

"Like hell!" Honestly questioning himself, he decided he'd tried hard as any man to forget the past, to be a different man. Trouble was, wasn't anyone else willing to see it that way. Almost with a vengeance he leafed back and forth through the pages until another, more suitable line caught his eye.

"*That which is crooked cannot be made straight . . .*"

"Now that," he said, "is the God's own truth." He slammed the Book shut, his thoughts bitterly cynical. What the hell was the use of trying anyhow? If he had an ounce of brains, he'd stick where he belonged, forget about trying to cross deadlines. What he ought to do is take up with Farley and his crew. They were men like him, outcasts with no loyalties and no ties. They'd end up with ropes around their necks or slugs in their backs, no one to notice and no one to give a damn. You couldn't buck fate and he'd been a fool to try.

As soon as he returned to the ranch, the Paiute sought out Jackson in the bunkroom. With a slight turn of his head, he motioned Jackson to follow. Outside, he again gestured Indian fashion with his chin, toward the barn.

He didn't speak until they got inside. When he did, Jackson for once in his life registered surprise. He'd never heard the breed string more than three or four words together at a time. Now his talk set easy and smooth as a hundred dollar saddle.

"I found Evans. Had an interesting conversation with that cowpoke."

"Your guns do the talking?"

He shook his head. "Matter of fact, I did some pretty close listening."

"Oh?"

"That's right. That cowboy tells a pretty convincing story."

"Most liars do."

"Yeah, well that's something you should know, Jackson."

Jackson's broad shoulders tightened. "Just what the hell you getting at, breed? This supposed to be a shakedown or something?"

"No, not at all. I just have a story of my own to tell and you better listen—close. Remember back this spring— Cedar City? You cached a wagon-load of rotgut and guns on the reservation while you looked for your buyer. As bad luck had it, some Paiute women and kids found it. You in turn found them and butchered every one of them . . ."

"So what's a few red hides got to do with the price of rice in China?"

Ignoring Jackson's sarcasm he went on as if he had never been interrupted, ". . . you butchered every one of them, but not before one of the women planted a knife between your ribs. That particular woman was the wife of the deputy marshal lawdogging that neck of the woods. That was a bad mistake you made, Jackson. But then you been making a lot of mistakes lately, ain't you?"

Jackson's eyes flickered in doubt.

Without change of expression, the Paiute nodded.

"That girl was my wife. A red hide to you, maybe. Some dirty little squaw. Well, she was my honest-to-God wife. And two of those kids were my baby girls.

"Jackson, my orders are to take you back to Cedar dead or alive. Now which way do you figger I'm going to do it?"

The challenge was plain. Jackson knew if he didn't make his try, the bastard breed would gun him down anyway!

Jackson's hand flashed to his gun. Shock twisted his face as he saw the Indian had him beat. *Not now! Not after all his careful planning!*

Three shots exploded, one on top of the other.

The Paiute slammed forward into Jackson, his shot going wild and throwing Jackson's off at the same time. When the Indian leaned unmoving against him, Maize tried to figure out what in hell happened. His own arms seemed to be all that held the breed on his feet. He held the man out at arm's length, and saw the bloody hole. Then, over the Paiute's shoulder he saw Bern, gun in hand. Pulling his arms away, Maize let the breed's body crumble to the dirt floor.

For a few moments Jackson just stood there, an involuntary shudder going through him. *God, that was close!*

Too unsure of his voice to chance speaking to Bern, Maize knelt by the breed's body and began rifling through his clothes. Under his shirt, pinned to the flannel undershirt beneath was the badge—*Deputy Marhsal* embossed across the top, *Territory of the United States* at the bottom.

Jackson swore. This really forced his hand. A missing federal officer could rain hell down on his head if it ever got traced back to him. He wondered if the breed had spilled his guts to Evans. Jackson tried to sort out his thinking.

The way things stood now, it was a toss-up which took priority—killing the cowboy or peddling Hensen's herd. Both had to be done. Whether he gained control of the 3-H or not, he still needed the income from Hensen's beef.

Regardless, that drive through the Canyon had to be made. The weather looked about right for it, too. First

162

thing come morning he'd send Bern ahead with word to Farley to bunch those cows and keep them ready to move at sign of the first snowflake.

Race, fixing his evening meal, turned from the stove as Kell Farley sidled through the doorway. Grooves of dissipation etched the surprised outlaw's face, but other than that, Race saw little change in Farley since their days together at the Laramie pen.

"Howdy, Kell. Food's about ready—bacon and pickles, unless you got something to add to the pot."

Farley stared at Race slack-jawed, awed as much by the cowboy's gall as the shock of seeing him there.

"What the hell do you call this!" he finally burst out.

Race set down the fork he'd been using to turn the bacon.

"That aint much of a greeting for an old friend, Kell."

"Ain't meant to be. What'd you expect after taking them potshots at me?" Farley stood legs spread, hands on hips close to his guns.

"Sure you don't have your spurs tangled, Kell? It's close to five years I laid eyes on you."

"I ain't got nothing tangled, damn you. You like to of killed me that night at Hensen's barn when you threw down on me. My arm's still sore where you creased me!"

"For hell's sake! Was that you? Say, Kell, I was bedded down in that barn when you fired it up. How the hell was I supposed to know it was you? I like to have got roasted alive in there if that fire ever really caught. But you didn't get killed and I didn't get roasted, so what the hell? Let's eat."

Farley at last responded to Race's casual indifference. "Yeah. What the hell. Shesty," he called out the door, "bring the flour and coffee in with you from outa the pack."

With the extra supplies, Race turned out a reasonable meal of flapjacks, bacon, coffee . . . and pickles.

As they ate, a sudden thought struck Farley and his eyes narrowed in suspicion. "How'd you find my place?"

"Didn't. It more or less found me. I'll level with you, Kell, I'm on the dodge."

"You ain't working for Jackson?" He still couldn't get it out of his head that Jackson had sicced Race onto him that night.

Race laughed shortly, without humor. "Not likely. He's one of the broncs I'm dodging—for now. He did a job on the Walker woman and the Mex who worked for Hensen at the house. Then he threw off the blame onto me. I need a hole and, well, I was thinking maybe you could use another hand. Hensen told me some about his deal with you and you might recall I'm a fair hand at running other men's beeves."

"How much of this Hensen deal do you know?"

"Not a hell of a lot. Hensen bought me, but I can't say he took me into his confidence. He offered me gun wages to work the cows into bunches to make it easier for you to gather. Way I understood it, he wanted to steal his own cows, split the take with you and cut the women out, get them thinking the outfit was about bust."

"Yeah, that's pretty much it. He didn't mention anything to you about the girl?"

"Who, his sister?"

"Uh-huh. I'm supposed to collect her, pretend we're holding her for—what the hell's that word, Shesty?"

"Ransom."

"Yeah, ransom. Then he lets on like he's got to sell off the rest of the outfit, buildings and all, to pay us off and get her back. Once the women think the outfit's gone under, he figgers they'll rattle their hocks outa there."

"Maybe you didn't catch it, Kell, but I told you the Walker woman's dead."

Farley shrugged. "Story's still good enough to hand his sister. Besides, you don't think that stupid son-of-a-bitch is really going to get anything back out of this run, do you? Just using that to keep him out of our hair while we make our gather."

Race relaxed a little. "Then you don't have any reason for going after the girl."

Farley cracked into a smile. "Well, for God's sake,

164

Evans, when did you become a Sunday School teacher? No reason?" he laughed. "A woman's good for more than collecting that ram—, ransom." He winked, the vacuous smile still on his lips.

When Race asked Farley about tying up with his outfit, he'd been dead serious, not seeing any other out for himself. But any doubts he had were gone. Whatever dust lay on his backtrail and whatever anyone else thought of him, he knew it just wasn't in him to trail with the likes of Farley. And if that little trash-mouthed bastard thought he was going to get his hands on Sage! Well, he'd hang around long enough to knock at least a few spokes out of Farley's wheels. Hensen's and Jackson's, too. Little chance he'd come through with a whole skin, but he didn't give a particular damn. Wasn't any future for him anyway.

"You got enough men to put this deal through, Kell? I just see you and your friend here."

Farley jabbed a thumb in the direction of his grubby companion. "Shesty here carries two irons and so do I. I figure just the two of us are the equal of any other four men."

"Sure enough, Kell, but guns don't drive cows. You need somebody knows cows."

Farley chewed on that thought. "You got a point there. Let's see . . ." he ticked off on his fingers, ". . . besides the two of us we got the Paiute, Bern, Stubbs, Jason, Stevens, and of course Jackson'll be around when we start the drive."

Shesty grunted aloud. "We haven't seen hide nor hair of Jason or Stevens and you'd better not count on Stubbs, neither."

"Why the hell not?"

"If you'd use your eyes as much as your mouth, you'd have noticed your long-lost pard here is wearing Stubbs' clothes."

Doubt pinched the little outlaw's forehead.

"How about it, Evans?"

Without volunteering additional information, Race told him, "Took them off a dead man. Never asked him his name."

165

From the look on Shesty's face, Race's answer didn't set well, but apparently it was enough to satisfy Farley. Kell shrugged it off. "If Stubbs's dead, what the hell difference who wears his clothes?"

He studied Race a long minute, thinking hard. Evans always treated him square at Laramie. Never poked fun at him about his size or nothing like some of the others. Always kept his mouth shut and minded his own business. But never let no one walk all over him, neither. Shesty was all right, but not too swift in taking orders. Evans would make a good hand to side him, especially in a showdown with Jackson.

"You want to take Stubbs's place?"

Race smiled, "Depends on how you mean that."

Farley laughed, clapping Race on the shoulder with one hand.

"You're okay, kid. Good to have you with us."

Again Shesty interfered. "Steppin' kinda fast, ain't you, Kell? Oughtn't you to talk this over with Jackson first?"

Farley's mood changed abruptly. Slamming his fist on the table, he swore. "Jackson's mapped out this deal, but I'm still running this outfit, Shesty, and don't you forget it."

Shesty snapped his mouth shut, pushed roughly away from the table and stomped outside.

Race had already figured that Jackson and Farley were in this together and he was glad to find out the two weren't exactly blanket-sharing buddies. Farley's outburst confirmed it and that was something worth remembering.

Once Shesty was out of hearing, Race said, "How about filling me in on details, Kell . . . where I fit in and where Jackson fits in. Don't forget that bronc is after my hide."

"That's right!" Farley smiled suddenly. "Well, here's the way she lays. We take Hensen's beeves—not to Lund where he usually sells or ships from, but not north, neither, where he thinks I've got a blind buyer. We're gonna take 'em straight south."

"South, but . . ."

Farley's smile broadened. "South. Straight through the Grand Canyon, to the railhead at Williams."

166

"*Through* the Canyon? C'mon, Kell! I seen that over-sized gopher hole. Ain't a man alive could navigate that horseback, let alone drive a bunch of cows down one side and up the other!"

"That's what most people think. But see, Shesty knows a trail. Look here—" Farley drew an imaginary arc on the table with his forefinger. "Going around the way everybody thinks you have to takes two hundred, two hundred fifty miles, most of it through the desert. But this trail cuts through the Canyon in a straight line. Whole trip from north to south rim ain't but thirty miles tops. Can you believe that!"

Race wagged his head while Farley went on.

"Shesty used to run small bunches of stole horses over this trail. Pick up a bunch in Arizona, sell 'em up in Utah. Turn right around, steal a bunch up there and sell 'em down in Arizona. I didn't know about it, but Jackson got talking to him one night and wormed it out of him. Figured out this deal to take over Hensen's herd. One thing about Jackson, he don't think small.

"Listen, kid, I'm gonna need help handling Jackson. You with me?"

"Against that bastard? You bet!"

"See, Jackson don't think I got him figgered, but I do. He's after 3-H hoof, hide and horns so he'll have a front for him to go after those Mormon herds. After he gets Hensen's beef, he'll try to cut me out. He don't have no intention of splitting with me. Trouble with Jackson is, he thinks he's so damn smart, he don't credit no one else with any savvy. Well, I don't have no big ambitions like Jackson, but I don't intend splitting the take on Hensen's herd with him, either. I want that money and once I get it, I'm off and running. This country's too damn cold."

"What do I get out of this?" Race asked, trying to sound interested.

"A quarter. Quarter for the other boys to split, and a half for me."

"Fair enough. Now how does the deal about the Hensen girl work—do we share that, too?"

Farley laughed. "The Paiute's go-between for Hensen

and me. He'll get word to us when Hensen wants it done. Kid, this's been the easiest deal I ever fell onto. Everybody's knocking himself out to hand me everything on a silver dish. Hot damn!''

Race turned his head to hide from Farley the reckless flare of disgust in his eyes. Inside a sense of urgency chafed at him. Maybe he'd made a mistake in trusting the Paiute. Sage might not be any safer with him than with Jackson or Hensen. Not a thing he could do but wait and try to get his hands on a gun.

Maybe the crooked can't be made straight, but this dog's hind leg is going to give it one hell of a run.

XXVIII

Recent events had unnerved Hensen. Like most of the others at Pipe Spring, he'd done too much drinking. Now, at home, he was doing too much thinking.

He was scared.

Not one of his old crew with him but Keno and he was out somewhere trying to locate the cows and make a count on them. He wasn't sure of this new hand Bern. Walker, Libby, Jésus . . . all three dead—killed. What the hell was to stop him from being next?

That was some surprise move Sage pulled, turning back her share of the ranch to him. He'd brooded over that, too, running hot and cold, elated one minute, worried the next, wondering why in the hell she did it. Walker's marker to Jackson wouldn't stand up in court. The ranch wasn't his to give. That share would revert to Sage, since Libby was her cousin, but not his. So even if she did give one share back to him, she still had a piece and if anything happened to him, she'd have it all.

He had no one—no wife, no children, no one to pass the fruits of his labors on to, no one except his half-sister Sage. Yet those were almost Sage's exact words and reasons for turning back her share. She'd said he was all the family she had, that the ranch meant nothing to her, that he was the real reason she had come here.

Maybe she really meant it. Come to think of it, she'd never asked for or demanded anything, never interfered, even helped the few times he let her. Any pushing been done around here was done by Jackson, supposedly on Sage and Libby's behalf. *Jackson.*

169

Had he killed Libby? At first he believed along with the others the drifter had done it. But now, he wasn't all that certain.

Evans had been with the women and Jésus better than a month, and Jésus and Libby spoke well of him. When pressed, Sage did too, but mostly she was reluctant to talk about him at all. A man would have to be pretty damn stupid to wait until the house was full of men to go ahead and kill a woman. And whatever else that cowboy was, he wasn't stupid. He'd saved the bulk of the 3-H herd while other ranches lost up to ninety percent of their stock already. And Evans caught onto his deal about robbing his own herds fast enough. Besides, what reason would the cowboy have for killing Libby and ravaging her like that?

Money? The drifter sold out to him fast enough. He could have just as well sold out to Jackson. *Jackson*. Back to him again.

Sage's turn-around complicated things. Three days ago, he might not have given a damn if she ended up like Libby. Three days ago he had no doubts, no questions—just an overriding resentment coupled with a determination to get back what was rightfully his, the methods be damned. Now he was in deep with men like Farley and Evans—rustlers, murderers, men whose services could be bought and traded around like bawdy-house tokens. Now the question gnawed at him—was he himself any better than the men he hired to squeeze a couple of women out?

With all this worry and cheap maneuvering, Hensen wondered if keeping the damn place was worth the trouble. Well, at least now he could call off his deal with Farley. He'd send word by way of the Paiute.

Where the hell was that breed anyway? He hadn't reported in, but he'd seen him earlier, heading for the barn with Jackson. *Jackson*. Damn, wasn't there anything went on around here that Jackson didn't have a hand in. Now he couldn't even trust the Indian. Hitting closer to home, even his own sister was tied too thick with that damn gunman.

Again Hensen thought of Libby's battered body and shuddered. Brotherly affection wasn't exactly bubbling out of the top of his head for Sage, but he sure as hell had no desire to see any woman end up like that.

Up to now he'd let things get past his control. Well, he'd get Sage the hell out of here, maybe even hire Farley to take her on up to one of the Mormon outfits while he came back here to square with Jackson once and for all. After that was taken care of, he'd decide exactly what, if anything, to do with his half-sister.

His own mind still wasn't clear on whether he needed to protect her or to be protected from her. But one thing sure as hell—he wasn't going to sit in a corner biting his nails till he found out.

The east sky was still dark, but the air was thick with flurries. Bern was already flying on his way to Farley with orders from Jackson. The big move was on.

Jackson lay back on his bunk staring through the blue haze that rose lazily form his cigarette. Things were fast boiling to a head and the old keen excitement rose up in him.

Soon all this would be his. Only thing in his way was that drifter and the Hensens. For now the drifter was beyond his reach, but the Hensen's were handy—just upstairs sleeping. The house was empty except for him and the Hensens. Maybe he'd been playing the game too cautious up to now. Why not slip up there, throw his gun and have done with it. Would save him the bother of making this drive under cover of a big snow. Wasn't likely any of Hensen's Mormon neighbors would come nosing around when the rancher didn't show come spring. Hensen sure as hell never went out of his way to cultivate the friendship of any of them.

The thought tantalized Jackson. Like the clouds of smoke rising from his quirly, his thoughts drifted then melded, always coming back to the same thing—get rid of Hensen and the girl now. Now, while the house is empty.

Slipping gun from leather, Jackson shelled the one empty chamber, checked the gun's action. He was about to kill another woman and somehow the knowledge exhilarated him. He thought about Libby. Too bad events broke the way they did. She was the only woman he ever wanted in that way. Well, he had her. What worried him was the way he'd lost control. He intended only to kill her. The other just happened. He wondered if it would be that way with Sage. He'd have to kill Hensen first to give himself time to find out. Anticipation is always half the fun of anything, anyway!

Like a stalking cougar he glided through the house, up the stairs, working from one room to the next.

He discovered the house was even emptier than he thought—Hensen and Sage slipped their hobbles and dodged out!

The three men idled the time away playing straight draw with a battered deck of fifty-one using matches as stakes. Race studied Farley and Shesty with amusement. They were playing like the matches were whittled out of gold and set with rubies. If he wanted, he could take those splay-fingered shorthorns for all they were worth—all twenty-three matchsticks apiece.

Unlike Jackson, Race made no show of being a gambler. But handling the pasteboards was like topping a bronc—once learned, never forgot. And what he had learned from Ruby Evans—namely every trick, dodge, and device for running a crooked game—he had learned well. As a kid, he had even experimented successfully with a few inventions of his own.

So while Farley and Shesty made their amateurish, obvious and only occasionally effectual attempts at manipulating the cards, Race returned the favor, just for the hell of it. He nail-marked choice cards, used the crimp and other false shuffles, and even second dealt a couple of times just to see if he could still do it. But even playing it straight, he was still way ahead of them so he slacked off to put them in a better mood.

As they played, Shesty loosened up a little giving Race a chance to pump him for information.

"Where at's this trail Kell's been telling me about? I

only been to the rim one time and couldn't see but one way of getting down in there—but since I ain't an angel with wings, I didn't try."

Shesty laughed, a rumble deep in his thick chest. "Nah. Due east of here's a lightning-struck tree—stripped bare except for one black arm juts out like a gallows. Looks like you come on to the edge of the world, but directly behind that tree's a cutback. That there's the head of the trail. Ain't much of a trail, I'll grant, but she gets the job done."

"How wide is it?"

"Anywheres from three to eight foot, except about a third of the way down. There's a kind of butte rim flattens out pretty wide, mebbe twenty-five, thirty feet there but only for about fifty yards and it narrows down again. Most of the way you got a sheer wall up on one side and a sheer drop on the other with only that narrow trail plastered to the side of a cliff like a mud-dauber's nest, the only thing between you and a trip to hell."

"Sounds fun, especially with snow to slick it up."

"Snow or not! Hell, first time I went over, I damn near browned my britches. Thought I'd get used to it after the first couple times, but I never did. That's why I quit. But this deal Jackson hatched up was too good to pass up."

"But what about the ice and snow?"

"Ain't the problem you'd think, except right near the top. Once you pass that, you got it made. Further you go down into the Canyon, the warmer it gets, like travelin' from Canada down into Mexico, know what I mean?"

Race nodded, then asked, "But don't you have to ford the Colorado to cross over to the south rim?"

"You do." Shesty's eyes narrowed. "But I don't tell no one where the crossin' is, not even Jackson. I gotta have some life insurance in this deal."

Farley looked annoyed by Shesty's remark, but Race saw the man's point. He could use some life insurance himself, preferably in the form of a six-shooter. Beyond scaring up one of those and waiting for the Paiute to show, Race had no clearcut plans. This waiting had him on edge—he was more worried about Sage than he wanted to admit. Even while they sat and played, his nerves screamed for him to quit camp and go find her. But the sensible thing to do for now was just sit tight, learn for sure where the Paiute stood.

Any kind of help along now would be appreciated. And if the Paiute weren't on the square and did deliver Sage to Farley, Race would still have a better chance of helping her than to go crashing around blind, dodging Jackson and Hensen.

So he lulled with the others, easing them off their guard while he primed himself for things to come, all the while waiting . . . waiting . . . waiting.

XXIX

Temperatures dipped further during the night and by morning a light snow started sifting down.

"Looks like this could be it!" Farley jounced on the balls of his feet like a man with the seven-year-itch and eight years behind on the scratching. "Bet we hear from Jackson any time now."

"You might be right. Here comes Bern now." Race let the burlap covering fall back across the cabin's lone window as he stepped away from it. "Loan me a gun, will you, Kell?"

Farley screwed up his eyes. "Ain't you the one told me you don't need a gun to drive a bunch of cows?"

"Dammit, he's Jackson's man," Race said. "All I want is an even show."

"You'll get it, but my way. Settle down. Let me and Shesty handle this."

Bern hauled up out front, threw off the reins and let his horse stand ground-hitched. Yellow slicker crackling as he tracked into the cabin, Bern stopped dead at sight of Race. Mouthing an obscenity, he dug under the yellow fish for his holstered gun.

"Hold it right there!" Farley's voice snapped from off to his left. At the click of Shesty's hammer to his right, Bern jerked spasmodically. Shesty and Farley had him whipsawed. Slowly he lifted his hand free.

"What the hell is this!"

"No trouble, Bern. Just didn't want you making no mistakes is all. Evans here is working for me."

Through tight lips Bern said, "Jackson ain't gonna like this—he wants this bronc dead."

Farley shrugged. "Tough. He can tell me all about it when he gets here. For now shuck your hardware and we can all relax."

Bern swore, but did as he was told. He knew Farley's unstable temper

Race said, "I'll look after his hoss." At Farley's nod, Race stepped outside. In the back of his mind lay the hope that Bern carried a saddle gun or even had an extra handgun stashed away in his saddlebags.

With a tinge of excitement, Race saw the rifle in the saddleboot—a Springfield .45-70. As soon as he led the animal around the corner where the side of the shack screened him, he flipped up the trapdoor of the singleshot only to find the breech empty. Keeping alert to anyone coming up on him, he quickly rifled through Bern's bags for shells. Not a damn thing there but .44's. Race swore. What the hell did Bern carry the carbine for, show?

With a sigh of disgust, Race led the horse the rest of the way to the pole corral and began stripping it down. Movement at the fringe of dark forest caught his eye. A shadowed figure emerged. Hensen, and on foot!

If, as Farley told him, the Paiute was go-between for him and Hensen, what was Hensen himself doing here? Hensen stopped and looked back over his shoulder. Was he being followed and where was his horse? It didn't make sense to Race. The rancher's step was crisp, so he hadn't walked far. His horse must be back in the woods a bit.

Race snapped his fingers! He'd bet his saddle against a silver dollar that Sage was back there. He'd bet that bastard had delivered the girl himself.

Race slapped Bern's saddle on his own buckskin and leading her from the corral, cut directly into the woods where Hensen had left them.

The pine was dense, but the snow made it easy for Race to backtrail the rancher.

Less than forty yards into the woods, Race won the silver dollar—sweeping aside the snow-heavy branches, he came face to face with Sage Hensen.

Sage had no idea why her brother had awakened her in the middle of the night, nor where he was taking her. After a cold two-hour ride, the last half hour in heavy snow, Hensen had finally pulled up, tied the reins of his bay to a branch and left her sitting there with only the admonition to *wait for me here*. He hadn't told her where he was going or why and she hadn't asked. She was too drained emotionally and physically to care.

But when Race made his sudden appearance, life snapped back into her. First she felt an involuntary surge of pleasure at seeing him again. Then she remembered. She remember Libby and Jésus and the promise she had made to herself.

The time that elapsed from the moment Race appeared until now was no more than an eye-wink. Her thoughts jelled and she reacted instantly.

Slashing her pony's flank with her quirt, she drove straight at Race. The animal's shoulder crashed against him, but in a blind grab at the pony's bridle, Race caught it.

Sage used her quirt again, but this time on Race, slashing at his hands and face. Protecting his still sensitive head with one hand, Race grabbed Sage's little leather whip by the poppers. He jerked hard and Sage, her wrist caught in the leather strap, twisted off the seat of her sidesaddle. Dangling helplessly by one knee around the curved iron brace of her saddle, she fought off Race.

His strong fingers dug into the softness of her arms as he tried both to support and control her thrashing body.

Shaking her once he whispered harshly, "Ease off, damn it!"

Claws out and back arched, she struggled even more violently to free herself. If it hadn't been for her woolen mittens, she probably would have taken one of Race's eyes out.

He shook her again until her teeth snapped.

"Listen, will you!"

"Listen to what, you murdering *tiger*! Libby and Jésus listened to you, but I know better!"

His eyes flicked and his face tightened, but he didn't

177

waste his breath on denials. He said, "Just quiet down and *listen*. Farley's camp is just ahead. Raise too much of a ruckus and you'll have him and his whole damn crew down on our necks. I'm quitting here and you're going with me."

"I wouldn't go anywhere with you—I'd rather face Farley than be dragged through the woods by a woman-killing Judas."

For the briefest moment his eyes reflected something Sage could not define, then they hardened.

"Think what you damn well please. It don't change a th—"

Gunshots broke out across the clearing, cutting off his words.

"Josh!" Sage screamed.

"C'mon!" Roughly Race shoved her back into the seat of her sidesaddle. Still holding her pony's reins, he mounted the buckskin and drove in his heels. Both animals plunged forward, urged by Race into a full run.

The racket of beating hooves and slapping branches drowned out Sage's cries for help.

As graceful as it was to look at, the sidesaddle left much in the way of practicality. With her right leg over the padded upper horn, resting just above her left leg, Sage barely managed to cling to the pony's mane with one hand. She leaned far over her mount's neck, and caught the cheek strap with her other hand. Pulling hard on the leather, she tried to force control of the animal away from Race.

From over his shoulder, Race saw what she was up to. Much as her antic slowed their progress, he had to admire her grit. But admiration or no, he swerved his buckskin into the pony, throwing the smaller animal off stride and nearly unseating Sage.

He drove the horses recklessly through the thick woods. Snow-covered boughs slapped at their faces and tore at their clothing keeping Sage from further defiance for the time being. He held that pace a full half hour before easing down to a ground-eating jog. Once he was sure the storm cut off pursuit by Farley or Hensen, he slowed the animals to a brisk walk, stopping occasionally to breathe the horses.

It was still daylight but barely so when they reached the west rim of the Canyon's easternmost gorge. Whipping winds beat needles of ice against them as they rode along the rim. As soon as Race found a likely spot, he pulled up.

Dismounting, he walked over to Sage, his limp pronounced. As he reached out to help her down, she lifted her hand, the handle of the quirt tightly gripped in her fist. Race looked directly up at her knowing she intended to use the whip on him again, but making no effort to move away.

Sage wasn't sure what stayed her hand. His appearance shocked her. He looked much as he did the very first time she had seen him—haggard, unshaved. But there was more. Evidence of Jackson's pistol-whipping still showed around his head. In addition red welts lay across his face in uneven relief where she lashed him earlier with the lead weighted poppers of her quirt.

She steeled herself against the sudden surge of pity, but she didn't use the quirt. Jerking her hand down to her side, she climbed out of the saddle, clinging to it until the weakness left her knees.

Race's heart went out to her as she leaned disconsolately against her pony. His hand half rose to her shoulder wanting to comfort her, to reassure her. But he pulled it abruptly back, suggesting, "Why don't you sit over there, between that clump of rocks while I set up camp?"

Without answering, she drew away from the pony and scrunched down in the shelter of one of the huge boulders and watched. Whatever else she thought of him, Sage had to admit to herself Race knew what to do and how to do it efficiently.

Shaking out a loop, he roped the top of a young sapling, pulled the top of the tree down until it nubbed up against a wind-gnarled juniper, then hitched the rope. He broke off evergreen boughs and stood them crosswind against the sapling. Once the crude lean-to was fashioned, he spread more of the boughs on the ground inside. Shaking out the tarpaulin from Bern's bedroll, he laid it over the pine branch floor. Setting the blankets over that, he folded the tarp back on itself into a rectangular bed. He snapped up the sides except for the last two rings.

He walked over to Sage and stood before her. "You'd better come on and try to get some rest."

"Take me back to my brother."

"I can't do that."

"If not tonight, then tomorrow . . . please!"

Race shook his head, lips clamped tight. How the hell could he tell this girl he couldn't take her back to her brother—that her brother conspired with a convicted woman-killer to do her out of her share of the ranch and he'd hired him for the same reason.

In a gentle voice he urged, "Come on. You'll lose your hands and feet to the frostbite if you don't get under shelter." That scared her into obeying and she let him tuck her in. In a show of consideration that surprised her, he slid a fire-warmed rock under the bottom tarp at her feet.

An overwhelming drowsiness enveloped Sage and just as she started to drift off, she felt a scuffling alongside her. Forcing her eyes open, she saw Race lift the left side of the bedroll and start to climb in.

She sat up abruptly. "What do you think you're doing!"

"Why, the same as you—looking to get a little shuteye without freezing my—without freezing to death. Any different ideas are yours, not mine."

"Well I'm certainly not going to sleep with you."

"Your choice, ma'am." Turning his back to her, he tilted his hat down over his head, pulled the covers up to his neck and was instantly asleep.

Doggedly Sage left the shelter. But ten minutes of the canyon's harsh updrafts drove her back to shelter, where she meekly climbed under the blankets beside Race.

When she awoke, she found herself warmly cuddled up to Race, her head cradled in the circle of his well-muscled arm. Shoving upright, a million blunt needles pricked at her flesh, a horrendous itching clawing at every point of her body. She groped wildly under her clothes and pulled out a handful of dried grass. Her first thought was where did dry grass come from in this storm. Her second thought dawned more slowly and more appallingly—how did it get under her clothes?

She looked at Race, who was watching her. Pushing up, he settled his hat on the back of his head and explained, "Temperature's dropped considerable and is still going down. Took the liberty of insulating your clothes."

"What other liberties did you take while I slept," she demanded.

Race's smile faded. "Well, now, what do you suppose?"

"I can only guess. There's nothing much beyond a man like you."

Angry now, his words drawled out thickly, "You're damned right—ain't nothing beyond a man like me!" Suddenly he grabbed Sage, and pulled her roughly across his chest. He forced cold hard lips against hers. The more she struggled, the harder he gripped her.

With a harsh laugh, he finally shoved her away and rose. "Figure for yourself how long you'd last out here if I was the kind of man you think I am."

Heart pounding fiercely, Sage fell back on the makeshift groundbed, her relief so great, she nearly fainted. When she regained enough composure to speak, she asked, "Then just what are you going to do with me?"

He shook his head. "I wish I knew."

"Race, for the love of God—"

"What the hell does a man like me know about God or love!" he flung back at her. "You're the only person in my life I ever spoke out my feelings to and you threw them right back in my face. Every chance you got, you rubbed my nose in my own dirt."

His laugh came out short and bitter. "Lady, you tell me—just what the hell do you expect of me?"

That was a question Sage had no answer for, either. Only after she lay there some time did the full impact of Race's words sink in. She burrowed under the covers and let the tears roll until she drifted into fitful exhausted slumber.

XXX

Maize Jackson had no idea where Hensen and Sage had
disappeared to, or what the rancher had in mind. With
Sage reverting her share of 3-H back to him, Hensen'd
have no call now to carry through on his deal with Farley.
With that part of his plan falling through, Jackson decided
to follow Bern on out to Farley's. Whatever else turned up,
he was determined to run off that herd and collect.

The going got rougher as the storm picked up, but
Jackson nevertheless made good time. Just a quarter mile
out from Farley's shack he heard the gunshots. Pulling his
horse to a halt, he stood in the stirrups and listened.
Suddenly his horse's ears twitched forward, at the same
time a horse ahead and maybe a hundred yards to the right
whistled shrilly.

Before his own horse could answer, Jackson leaned
forward and clamped down hard on its muzzle. He dismounted then, cautiously leading his horse in the direction
of the other. Soon he came upon Hensen's empty-saddled
bay among the pines, its trailing reins snagged to a downed
branch.

In a rush he remounted then circled through the woods
to reach the corral back of the cabin.

Because Farley's shack had only that window at the
front, Jackson approached from the other side, reaching
the door unseen. The door stood wide open on its leather
hinges. Peering through the crack he saw Bern standing
alone in there, a butcher knife in his hand.

"It's Jackson, Bern. I'm coming in."

"Whew! Am I glad to see you!"

"What the hell's going on?"

"Boss, I'm not so damn sure my ownself."

"Tell it from the start."

"Minute I got here, Farley and Shesty whipsawed me, took my gun away. That bronc you been after—Evans—was hiding out here. Farley says he's workin' for him. Well, Evans goes out to put my horse up, he says. Next thing I know, in walks Hensen. He tells Farley their deal is off. He looked like he wanted to say more, but Kell wouldn't have none of it. Then everything happened so fast I couldn't follow it. To tell the truth, without no gun, I dove under the table.

"Farley shot Hensen, but the old man made tracks before Kell could finish the job. Him and Shesty took out after him and I don't have no idea at all what happened to Evans."

"I saw Hensen's bay back there in the woods. Come on!'

Jackson and Bern tore across the clearing into the woods. But when they reached the scuffed-up area, it was empty. Swearing out loud, Jackson ran back to the clearing and fired his gun three times. Farley and Shesty came on the trot.

"Did you get him?" Jackson asked.

"I plugged him a second time, but he still got away."

"All right, all right. Forget about him now. First give Bern his hardware back. You and me are going to have some settling up to do later, Kell, but I'm letting things slide for now. It's more important to get those cows moving—this's the storm we've been waiting for!"

Moving the cattle in a snowstorm wasn't the great idea Jackson figured it to be. Like the rest of the crew helping him, he was a gunhand, not a cowboy.

The damn stupid critters insisted on drifting before the storm, little bunches breaking off here and another there. Up until today, the men had worked only small bunches at a time. Now they were trying to handle close to a thousand head of cattle plus a scattering of twenty or so horses.

A couple of hours of this were enough for Jackson.

"You men keep working the cattle. There are a bunch of other things I have to tend to. I'll load up supplies on a couple of packhorses. You scatterbrains should have had that all taken care of instead of warming your rumps by the fire. Bern, help me catch up a couple of those geldings. When I get the packs together, I'll go right on down the trail to that little plateau you told me about, Shesty."

"You can't miss it—the Tonto's the only wide spot in the trail, about half-way down, just under them real steep redwalls. There's some pretty good springs and caves up in the redwall, but no place to bed down the cows until you hit that platform."

Jackson frowned. He didn't relish the thought of bedding down with a bunch of cows overnight. "I just might go right on down and meet you by the river. See you when you get there."

When Sage awoke the second time, it was morning, but a dark day filled with snow. Race hunkered by the fire cooking chunks of meat on a green stick. Seeing her stir, he offered her a piece. It had been more than twenty-four hours since she'd had a bite to eat—the longest she'd ever gone without eating in her life—and she took the food without hesitation.

As soon as she downed that, Race offered her another.

"Deer meat?" she asked. At his nod, her eyes skimmed the camp. She was starved and believed she could eat half a deer by herself. "Where's the rest of it?" she asked.

"That's all there is." Seeing the question in her eyes, he added, "Found what was left of a cougar kill."

The chunk of meat lodged in her throat, unwilling to go down and unable to come up.

"Here, drink this." Race handed her a curved piece of bark with some kind of liquid in it. This time she did hesitate.

"What is it?"

"It's all right," he assured her. "Just boiled some spruce needles in snow water. Kinda tastes like tea."

Sage drank it reluctantly, thinking what a sorry pass she

184

had come to. Her clothes were barely more than rags after that rough ride. As a matter of fact, Race had sometime during the night torn off pieces of one of the blankets and wrapped them around her feet. And here she was gulping wild food and lapping her drink like some animal. She looked at Race and realized what it must have been like for him when she first met him. Then that night when she refused him the leftovers. Knowing what a fierce pride he had, it was a wonder he had tolerated her arrogance as well as he had. Suddenly her eyes filled with tears.

"Oh, Race. Things could have been so different. Why did you have to kill Libby and Jésus!"

"You really believe that, don't you?"

"I've never heard you deny it."

He looked at her intently, a hard bitterness on his face that she had never seen before.

"If I have to deny a thing like that to you, why then I guess I don't give a damn what you think. But there's one thing I'd like you to tell me. Did you ever ask Jackson to deny it?" As soon as he asked the question, an invisible curtain dropped over his face and he became utterly remote.

There was no use asking him what he meant by that. But why should she ask Jackson. It was Race she found kneeling by Libby's body. But Jackson had been there, too.

Where did he come from anyway? She tried to reconstruct the scene in her mind. The door to the storeroom was hinged so that it opened inward. That was in case of snow, they'd still be able to open it. She had come down the steps, turned toward the storeroom. There was Race kneeling by Libby. He turned his face to her. In a flash of recall, she remembered the look on his face. At the time, she thought it was the shock of being discovered. But now, she saw it as being twisted with grief.

He had reached out his hand to her and the next thing she remembered, she was on him clawing and kicking. Then Jackson came from behind and started pistol-whipping . . .

From behind! There was no way Jackson could have

gotten behind Race except from the storeroom. Could he have been hiding behind the door?

That was Libby. But what about Jésus? Jackson had been *there*, too.

Sage looked at Race wanting to ask him questions, but that unseen barrier he set up was still there and there was no approaching him. He'd closed her off.

Wordlessly Race began breaking camp and, in a curiously subdued frame of mind, Sage helped him.

Race didn't know the country well enough to go slamming around blind in a blizzard so he decided the safest thing to do for Sage was find the trail Shesty told him about. If nothing else, it would get her down out of this bitter cold.

Mid-morning and he still hadn't found the trail. Maybe Shesty had lied. Just as he was about to give up, Race saw the lightning-struck tree.

When he got close enough to the blackened tree to see the cutback on the canyonside, Race also saw something else that caused him to draw up his horse so sharply that Sage's pony ploughed into the back of it.

Three men rode out of the woods at the same time—*Farley, Shesty,* and *Bern.*

XXXI

Race's heart sank as he saw Farley and the others. He'd hoped above all things to avoid a meeting with them or Hensen or Jackson. Too late now and nothing for it but to cozen them along until he saw a chance to safely cart Sage out of this jackpot.

He hated to open his mouth, knowing each word would further damn him in her eyes. But he had no choice.

As he spoke, the south Texas drawl hung thickly, each word coming out like two.

"Kell," he said, acknowledging the other two at the same time with a curt nod of his head. "Had a hell of a time finding this place. Wasn't due east like I'd been told." He cast a dark look in Shesty's direction.

Farley glanced at Shesty, too. "No wonder you was so sure Evan's wouldn't show." He turned again to look at Race. "See you managed to pick up my bonus, too."

"Yeah, well I was out there tendin' Bern's hoss when I saw Hensen cutting shank's mare from the woods to the cabin. Figured from what you told me, the girl might be back there. She was, sure enough. I'd no sooner come up on her, when it sounded like hell settin' up store in the preacher's parlor. What happened anyway?"

"Hensen tried to commit suicide."

Hearing Sage's gasp at his side, and wanting to head her off from asking questions, Race prodded, "He dead?"

"If he's not, he should be. Plugged him a couple of times but he got away. He wanted to call off our deal—"

"No call to go into detail, Kell."

"Why not? Afraid of upsetting the little lady's tender

187

feelings?'' A hungry smile on his lips, Farley kneed his horse stirrup to stirrup with Sage, sandwiching her between himself and Race. ''You want to know all about your brother, don't you? How he hired me to rustle his own cattle and split with him so he could cut you and that other calico skirt out. You want to know how he hired me to keep you with me for a few days, so he could pretend he had to sell his outfit to come up with ransom money.

''That was the deal. Then yesterday he come crying how he's changed his mind. Like hell! A deal's a deal. Just a good thing my old pard was handy. Knew I could count on Evans to come through for me one way or another.'' He nudged his horse even closer to Sage and ran his hand over her as if he were examining a piece of horseflesh.

''Plenty of time for that later, Kell. It's getting late and I'd like to know what the deal is from here on out.'' The expression on Race's face remained bland, giving nothing away of what he felt, but the words came out in a drawl markedly thicker. Holding his gaze steady on Farley, he caught Sage from the corner of his eye. She was watching him and looked to be fighting back a smile. His insides turned to ice, damned if the poor girl hadn't come un-hinged!

But Sage actually had better command of herself and her feelings than at any time since she first butted heads with Race Evans. There were so many things about the man she had always refused to accredit and suddenly they all crystallized.

She realized he could have told her about Josh earlier and made himself look good in her eyes. But rather than throw a shocker like that at her, he'd kept quiet, just refusing to take her back to her brother without telling her his reason for it.

More importantly, whatever his relationship with these men, she knew with absolute certainty she was safe from them as long as Race was around. She still wasn't certain whether he was responsible for Libby's and Jésus' deaths, but she doubted it. In any case, she admitted to herself it just didn't matter. *She loved him.*

The one thing that triggered recognition of these truths

188

was the same thing that had provoked the grin—the thing that always gave him away—that fool south Texas accent of his. She almost laughed aloud.

Race looked full at her, pity in his eyes. Tough for her to learn the truth about her brother that way. Damn Farley anyway! If he had to blab, why the hell wasn't it Jackson he called the ticket on! Too late now—or was it? A small grin formed at the corners of his lips.

"Has Jackson made contact with you yet?"

"Yeah. He come out to the shack. Ordered us to start moving these cows. But you notice soon as the going got rough, he cut out. Supposed to meet him somewhere down below. Hell, he's got all the supplies and we're up here in the ice and snow trying to move a bunch of rustled cows for him." Farley hesitated. "We got a little problem there, kid."

"How's that?" Race asked, glad to get the little outlaw's mind on something else besides Sage.

"You was right. We don't know a damn shucks about moving that many cows at once. We were just gonna go on down the trail now to hunt up Jackson and tell him we couldn't do it."

"Well, I'll tell you, Kell, you don't move that beef today, you might as well forget about them. If you don't take 'em, this storm or the canyon will."

"How do you mean?"

"They'll drift before the storm. If there's a fence, they'll pile up in front of it till you got a bridge of dead bodies and the ones coming up from behind will walk right over it. If there isn't a fence, they'll just keep on till they reach the rim. The push of cattle coming up from the rear will drive them on over. Cows are raised for their steaks, not their brains, don't forget."

"So that was it? We kept trying to head 'em east, but they drifted like we wasn't even there."

"Well, if they haven't got too far, we can still handle them if you do what I say. The girl can help. She worked cattle with me in that last storm."

Just like that, Farley acceded the leadership to Race and in the same stroke, Race made certain Sage would be in his sight at all times.

They found the cattle, about seven hundred of them. In quick appraisal, Race saw the task would be difficult, but not impossible for men who knew shucks about working cattle.

Signalling for the others to follow suit, he dismounted and with a twig began describing in the snow how they would work it.

The old she-cow he'd been looking for was heading out the herd. "Sage, you take point right in front till we get these leaders slowed and give the drags a chance to catch up." He looked at her, hoping she'd cooperate and not do anything to draw extra attention to herself. As if sensing this, she nodded.

"Bern, you flank 'em over there on the right, keep them strung out. Kell, you push the drags, but not too fast so they don't take into sulling, hear? Both of you, don't let those cows bunch up. Shesty, you and me will trade off hosses for just a little while. I'm going to catch up that old brindle she-cow and snub her up to your saddle, then we'll trade back and you'll go on point."

"Why do I have to go first?"

"You're the only one knows the trail, remember? Now when you take up point, instead of riding dead front, drop back to here." He marked a point at a forty-five degree angle off the leaders. "Once Shesty's in position, we'll start turning them slow. Remember we don't have a remuda, so ride easy and don't wear your hosses down with a lot of useless motion. Once we get them turned, walk your hoss through the cows at an angle till you're on the left. The Canyon'll be on their right then and that should keep those cows honest. Any question?"

If there were, no one voiced them. "Okay, then take up your positions and we'll get cracking while we've got enough daylight to work with."

By dusk they had only reached the head of the trail. With genuine disgust, Race conceded that Sage made a better hand than those other three put together.

190

"Pull up! We'll have to bed them here for the night. Don't think there's a one of us wants to risk driving seven hundred cows over that tightwire Shesty calls a trail—not in the dark. All right, let's circle 'em.''

Ordinarily, Race would have had a herd twice that size bedded down in half the time and the continuing snow only made matters worse. The inconsistent handling and the night winds made the herd snuffy.

"We'll have to take turns standing night guard. Kell, you and Bern work the first while Shesty and me set up camp. Shesty, butcher out a calf.''

With Sage helping, Race set up camp in no time. Tonight there'd be no sharing of blankets with Sage. He'd put Shesty and Farley on first night guard—he wanted to get that little bastard so tired he wouldn't even want to think of Sage—so he could use their soogans.

When he called the others in to eat, he told off their watches. "Cows are too spooky for one man to handle tonight and we don't have enough hands to go two-hour tricks. So Kelley, you and Shesty take the first guard four hours. Bern and me'll stand the midnight to dawn.''

Kell Farley complained until Race pointed out the second watch would run a couple of hours longer than the first.

Sometime during the second watch Sage was startled awake by a hand clamping over her mouth. Eyes opened wide, she discovered Bern, a finger lifted to his lips enjoining her silence.

Relief flooded her. At first she thought it might be Farley. But Bern seemed like a decent enough puncher the few days he spent at the ranch.

He leaned over and whispered in her ear.

"I know where your brother is. He's bad hurt and needs you. If you want, I'll take you to him.''

At her slight hesitation, he added, "He did back out on his deal with Farley, you know.''

Sage nodded. "Take me to him.''

Quietly Bern led her away from the fire, across the flat to the woods. "Got our horses hobbled in there,'' he explained.

By now they were out of sight and sound of the camp and in a sheltered area. A small fire was going and a blanket lay stretched out on the ground.

Sage turned to ask, "Where are the hors—"

Before she had a chance to finish her question, Bern wrestled her down onto the blanket. His eager mouth spread over hers.

The quickness, the unexpectedness of Bern's assault threw Sage into a panic. As hard as she tried to nerve herself up, her muscles refused to act with any strength or direction. While she struggled helplessly under his weight, Bern whispered into her ear, "Fight all you want, honey! The wilder the colt, the better the ride."

Suddenly Sage felt Bern's weight torn from her—heard the sodden thuds of fist meeting flesh. The next thing she was aware of were hands lifting her, trying to steady her on nerveless legs.

"It's all right. You're all right." It was Race.

"Oh, thank God!" Her legs nearly went out from under her again and she began shivering uncontrollably.

"It's all right," he said again. "When I missed Bern on circle, I backtracked him."

As Race stood with his arm around Sage, bracing her up, Farley came crashing into the clearing. Looking from Race to Sage, he drew his gun.

"No wonder you wanted the long shift, damn you!"

"Ease off, Kell. Look over there." Race tilted his head in the direction of Bern, who was only now beginning to struggle to his feet. "Had to explain to your boy over there that this piece of calico is your own private property."

Farley's eyes, following the shift of Race's head, saw Bern.

"He ain't my boy. He's Jackson's."

Turning his gun on Bern, Farley fired three times rapidly, then said, "Now he's the devil's."

XXXII

Until now, the storm had been nothing worse than heavy snows tossed around by the Canyon's updrafts. But by dawn all this changed into a full-fledged norther. Gale winds drove sub-zero temperatures even deeper. Miniature icicles formed on the cattle's eyelids and clung to their hides. The herd was up and moving and in spite of Race's best efforts, they turned. Those cows would drift now and nothing short of death could stop them.

They had to let the cattle go. They'd already wandered off too far from their landmark themselves, trying to turn the damn herd. From here on out, it would be a struggle just to keep themselves alive. The air was so thick, their horse's heads in front of them were dim gray shadows.

Riding strung out, ropes tied from saddle horn to saddle horn against losing each other, they searched frantically for the fire-blackened tree and the trailhead hidden behind it.

With a cowboy's ingrained distrust of paint horses, Race wouldn't let Sage ride the pinto pony down into the Canyon. Appropriating Bern's horse for himself, he put Sage up on his buckskin. Not giving a damn for amenities, he'd forced her into Bern's trousers and slicker and made her ride the mare astride. He looked back at her now, but couldn't see her for the snow. He ran his hand along the tautness of the rope between her horse and his, just to asure himself she was still there.

In a brief moment they had together that morning, she told him about reverting her share of 3-H to Hensen. If her brother were still alive, he'd at least no longer pose a threat to her.

The pressure of what almost happened to Sage in the predawn darkness rode heavy on Race. He'd played the wait-and-hope game almost too long. He had to act and he took the time now to figure their chances.

With Hensen out of the running one way or the other, they still had this killing blizzard on top, Jackson down below, and Farley and Shesty in the middle to contend with. Damn poor odds no matter how you cut it. And the odds on cutting down those odds were even poorer with nothing but his wits and Jésus' knife to do the job with.

He'd just have to take it a step at a time. Trouble was this looked to build to one hell of a long trip for someone.

Just then he felt the rope between him and Kell slacken off. Shesty'd backed his horse up to Farley and Farley'd followed suit, so that the three men were side by side and shouting against the wind.

"I found it! Can't see the trail, though. We'll have to go it blind!"

"The hell we will!" Farley said. "I'm gonna set right here."

"Getting down into the Canyon is the only real chance we've got, Kell," Race said. "We're damned if we do, and damned if we don't—but maybe a little less damned if we make the try."

"Well, I'm not going down tied up like this. What if Shesty's hoss loses its footing? Hell with that kind of thing."

"Either we go tied together or by damn I won't lead you down!" Shesty argued back.

What Farley said gave Race an idea—not an idea he'd be proud to talk about later. Just thinking about it gave his mouth a sour metal taste. But there was nothing on God's earth he wouldn't do to get Sage through this, even to keep her alive a little longer.

He backed up Shesty. "Nothing's changed, Kell. Shesty knows the trail. You're a lot better off tied to him than you would be batting around blind on your own. And don't forget, *your* hoss could just as easy lose *its* footing."

Weighing benefits against risks, Farley yielded.

Nodding, Race said, "Let me drop back and tell the girl."

He backed Bern's horse gently until he could make out the garish flare of Bern's yellow slicker. Sage was huddled so low in it, he could hardly make out her face. Leaning far over in the saddle, his lips almost touched her ear as he explained the situation. Then he added,

"When you feel the rope between me and you slack off, pull back on the reins. Buck'll stand. Just keep her there and don't move until I come and get you. If something happens that I'm not back in fifteen minutes, do your best to follow the trail the rest of the way down into the canyon. Just give the mare her head—if there's a way to make it, she'll find it."

He rubbed the buckskin between the ears. "She's a damn fine hoss."

As he kneed Bern's bay forward, the play in the rope signalled the others to move on out. The trail offered nothing to build their confidence. It was a narrow, snow-choked, frozen slice of hell. Wind-driven sleet scoured their faces, battered and numbed their senses. Their lives depended entirely upon the instincts and surefootedness of the animals they were riding.

That's when Race made his move.

He laid back enough on the bay to slacken the rope between him and Sage—enough to unwind the dallies and untie the end from his saddlehorn. He let the rope drop free, trusting Sage to carry out his instructions.

Hitching up his left leg, he lifted the saddle fender to get at the girth beneath. What he was attempting was chancy at best, but their only hope as he saw it. He loosened the cinch a notch and then, taking a deep breath, he grabbed the horn with both hands. Leaning to the right, with his left leg free, he dropped all his weight—for just an instant—into the right stirrup. As the saddle started giving to that side, Race jumped free, crashing into the towering inner wall of the trail.

His jump sent the loosened saddle under the bay's belly throwing the animal into a bucking fit. It thrashed crazily to rid itself of the dangling rig. It's rear hooves caught Race in mid-air knocking him over the narrow ledge.

Clawing desperately, Race hooked the protruding root of a scrub cedar with one hand. For the slowest-moving moment of his life, he swung like a pendulum out of control, scraping and banging against the cliff's rocky face. By the sheer strength of his grip and arm, he clung to the side of the sheer overhang, then gradually, muscles straining, dragged himself back up onto the shelf.

A pandemonium of human and animal shrieks reached out to him, the terror in their screams stamping a permanent brand on Race's soul. As a sudden blast of icy wind cleared the air, he watched the havoc he created, whitefaced and shaken.

Farley's ankle somehow got bound up on the rope between his oversized gelding and the bay Race had been riding. He hung like a rag doll, screeching in pain as his head and shoulders bounced helplessly against the ground. Just then Shesty kicked free of his horse. The thrust of that man's body sent his animal plunging over the edge. In a chain reaction, it carried Farley's horse over, then Farley, and finally the bay.

The thick air closed around them once more. In wild panic, Shesty began scrambling back up the trail. He barrelled through the snow haze into Race, literally running over the cowboy. Race couldn't let the outlaw get past him. In his state of mind, Shesty would drive the buckskin right off the ledge and Sage with it. From the ground Race's hand flashed out and caught Shesty by the heel. As Shesty tried to jerk free, the sharp rowel of his spur tore a gash down Race's hand, but he hung on.

Twisting back to face him, Shesty set the heel of his other boot on Race's hand, trying to scrape it off. As he dragged his foot down, the rowel of the one spur hung up in the shank of the other. Shesty's body wrenched off balance. Arms flailing, he disappeared over the narrow rim trail, his empty spurred boot still in Race's hand, his empty screams echoing back.

Rubber-kneed, Race hauled unsteadily to his feet. Dropping the boot, he rubbed his hand against his pants-leg, then staggered to the protection of the inner wall, leaned against it and was sick. Once braced up, he examined his hand. A deep slash ran from the base of his thumb to his wrist. Wrapping his kerchief around the injured hand, he walked stiffly back to Sage, his body one huge aching bruise.

When Sage saw Race coming toward her, her relief was so great, she jumped off the buckskin and ran to him. She slipped on the loose gravel, but Race caught her before she fell. With his arms around her, standing close, she looked up at him. The haunted look on his face shocked her. She started to ask him what happened, but the warning shake of his head stopped her and she realized that was one question she would never ask.

Trembling, she buried her head against his chest, tightened her arms about him as great sobs shook her body.

"Oh, Race, I was so afraid."

"Everything's all right now. You're safe."

"I wasn't worried for me. I couldn't stand it if something had happened to you . . . especially without your ever knowing . . ."

"Knowing what?" He held her away from him so he could see her face.

She looked up at him. "Without your knowing that I love you." Her statement didn't have the impact on him that she thought it would. He gave her a wan smile, shaking his head. After a long drawn-out silence, he pulled her to the base of the cliff wall and sat her down. Wearily he dropped beside her.

Taking one of her small hands in his, he studied it a moment before finally speaking.

"Sage, a man who's been in prison likes to kid himself that he can pick up his life right where he left off. It just don't work that way. You just had a pretty good scare. Right now you're in a situation you're not equipped to handle, you have to depend on me—on a man's strength— to pull you through. But nothing's really changed. Our chances of getting back on top whole meat aren't very good, but if we do, I'll still be what I was—an out-of-work bronc-snapper. And in back of that I'll still be an ex-con—a *tiger*." A faint smile softened the harshness of his words. "Sage, I look pretty big to you right this minute, but back on top—well, just tell me what the hell need you'd have for a man like me."

"What need does a woman have for any man—for that special man?"

He shook his head and started to speak, but she laid her fingers across his lips. "Race, I've used those same arguments on myself a dozen times, ever since the first time we squared off against each other down at the barn. There were times after Libby and Jésus were murdered that I hated myself, because, even believing you had done it, I still cared. Nothing you say can change my mind. Unless it's just that I've killed off any feeling you might have had for me?"

"God, Sage, don't—"

He pulled her to him, cradling her in his arms, her small head nestled under his chin. Looking past her into the future, he knew chances were that twenty-four hours from now, neither one of them would be alive. But if they survived he knew he'd do anything to keep her love. His arms relaxed and he held her away from him to look at her again. Brushing her forehead with his lips, he said, "Come on, we still have a long way to go."

Race rose gingerly, favoring his battered body. When Sage insisted he ride the buckskin, he lifted her onto the saddle ending that argument. Leading the mare, he tucked his head against the wind and started down the trail, hugging the inner wall.

As they descended, the snow thinned, and finally disappeared. As if nature feared making things too easy for them, the trail narrowed further—pitching so steeply, the mare almost rode its own haunches.

The precarious trail led into another deeper canyon of vertical upthrusts and jagged black rock. Ugly, foreboding, it looked like hell after the fires burned out. To cross here, they had to travel across a long bridge, barely the width of the buckskin. No protective wall to cling to existed here—just a tenuous obsidian spine with sheer drops of several hundred feet on each side. Gusts of wind pushed and tugged at them as they crossed and after what seemed two lifetimes, they made it.

Another switchback brought them to a perpendicular gorge. A wall rose on their right to a height of several hundred feet. On their left, unbroken palisades plunged a thousand feet to meet the raging red river below—the Colorado.

Both breathed audible sighs of relief as the trail cut back in again, away from the river. As they angled sharply at a vee in the trail, a familiar sardonic figure blocked their path.

Race swore bitterly. In his state of battered exhaustion he'd forgotten all about Maize Jackson.

XXXIII

A gun appeared magically in Jackson's hand. He looked at Race and shook his head.

"Well, Evans. Never had you figured for a stayer in this game. After all, I had the deck stacked and dealt before you ever took a hand. That's all right, though. I always did like a little competition to liven up the play."

"Competition, hell! That what you called Libby and Jésus when you killed them? This isn't a game of cards and a pot to be won!"

"Isn't it? It's all just one big game of *freezeout*. And when there can be only one winner, you just got to expect a lot of losers."

In a flash of insight Race prompted, "Sage's parents?"

"Sure. Took Libby in for supplies, left her at the hotel. I backtracked to camp. Had the old man's 'will' already rigged up—forgery happens to be one of my better developed, if lesser known talents. After I put the old man and his wife out of their misery, I planted the paper, got back to the hotel and even managed to catch a couple hours of sleep.

"Figured to work the rest of it through Libby. When we got to the 3-H the set-up was even better than I hoped for. I saw a chance not just for a quick clean-up like I first thought, but a chance to rake in a really big pot. Libby nearly fouled things up when she married that bag of sheep dung. But things worked out fine right up to and including now. I mean, here you hand-deliver the last tie-up to me." He pointed to Sage.

"Like hell, Jackson!"

Jackson laughed. "Face it cowboy. You're holding a busted flush."

There was no way Race could argue that. With Jésus' knife tucked down inside his boot, Jackson would have him spit, drawn, and over the fire before he could ever reach it.

Sage, momentarily forgotten by the two men, stared at Jackson. The enormity of all Jackson had done filled her with a roiling hate. For the first time in her life, she had an overpowering desire to kill—to destroy.

Without calculating the risk to herself, she suddenly gigged the buckskin, drove him along the narrow shelf past Race, straight at Jackson.

The unexpectedness of her move startled both men. Jackson flung himself against the wall. As the buckskin brushed against his gun arm, its hind leg left the edge. Race tried to yell, but his throat felt as if someone crammed ground cactus into it.

Sage made it safely around, but his fear for her almost cost Race the one chance her rash act had given him. Snapping to life, he swept Jésus' cuchillo from his boot.

Jackson already was up on his feet, reaching for the gun the charging buckskin knocked from his hand. Race got there first and kicked it over the rim. As the gun clattered down the corrugated slope, its hair-trigger exploded off a shot.

Then in one of his unbelievably quick moves, Jackson pulled his Bowie. The murderous weapon sported a fourteen-inch blade of tapered steel, razor sharp. Its three-inch backcurve was just as lethally honed and the length of the weapon gave Jackson added reach.

He lunged at Race, slitting the sleeve of his heavy sheepskin coat and drawing blood. But as Jackson came at him, Race flicked his own steel catching a slice off Jackson's wrist.

Cursing, Jackson marked two things about Race in that instant—the cowboy was a southpaw and he was an experienced knife-fighter.

As they parried, they noted each other's weaknesses.

Race's left-handedness threw off Jackson's rhythm, forcing openings the killer ordinarily would not yield. In turn, Jackson played his superior mobility against Race's game leg.

Everything each man ever wanted was at stake here and, like the storm-driven cattle, nothing short of death could stop them. A fight like this allowed no margin for error. With that knowledge prompting both men, the fight took on a slow and cautious tempo as they faced off on the narrow ledge, one the mirror image of the other, their bodies turned sideways to offer the smallest possible targets.

Jackson feinted then sliced at Race's middle. The forestroke cut away the entire front of Race's coat. On the backstroke he twisted his wrist so that the concave arch on the back of the knife caught at Race. Only a savage sucking in of his belly kept the cowboy from being disembowled.

Backpedaling, Race drew Jackson off by jabbing at his face with his bare right hand, then stroked rapidly with the knife in his left. Jackson drew back swearing. His coat hung in shreds and his body burned under numerous slits.

Race stroked again, missed. He blocked Jackson's thrust with his free hand, and in the exchange slammed the shaft of the double-edged cuchillo under Jackson's jaw. The killer stumbled backwards, stunned. When Race tried to press his advantage, Jackson sliced upward ripping sleeve and flesh off Race's right forearm.

They sparred some more with tentative thrusts and feints, each trying to force the other into a fatal mistake. Their clothes hung in tatters, their torsos a grid of slits and gashes. Each move showered a spray of sweat-diluted blood.

Race's controlled style of fighting wore on Jackson's patience. He pressed recklessly, hoping to draw Race into a sucker move. But knife fighting was Race's game as much as Jackson's and he didn't draw. He continued his methodic blade work slicing, stroking, small hits that drew more and more blood.

Fear of bleeding to death threw Jackson into a frenzy.

All caution aside, he lunged at Race. When Race brought his steel up against Jackson's, the killer closed with him. His free fist pummeled Race's bruised side where he'd slammed against the canyon wall earlier. In the half-clinch, Race dug the knuckles of his free hand into Jackson's kidney. Jackson yelled, and in desperation caught his heel behind Race's bad leg and jerked it out from under the cowboy.

As Race crashed to the ground, he pulled Jackson with him, lifting his good leg between as they came down, somersaulting Jackson over his head.

When they dragged to their feet, their positions were reversed, Jackson now on the upper tilt of the trail. Backstepping downhill put Race at a decided disadvantage with his bad leg. Jackson lost no time in catching this. He jabbed his long knife forward, again forcing Race to backpedal. Going on the offensive, he forced the action to Race, forcing him backwards until the cowboy lost his footing on the loose shale.

Race fell backwards, landing with his head hanging over the bleak nothingness. Neck muscles corded as he strained to keep his head up, to bring his dangling right arm and leg back onto the solidness of the shelf.

Jackson dived on top of him, but had to pull short as Race brought up his knife and locked it against the guard on Jackson's. Twisting slightly, Race wrapped his free-swinging leg around Jackson. If he went over, he'd damn well see to it that Jackson went with him.

The threat of that yawning gorge forced Jackson to change strategy. He dragged himself as far back from the rim as possible, taking the tenaciously clinging Race with him.

Their steel blades grated against each other and soon Jackson realized Race had superior power as the knives inched closer to the killer. But Jackson had superior weight and now he put it to use. Pushing up onto one knee, he laid the full bulk of his body behind his knife hand. For long minutes they remained locked that way until Race's arm began to yield to the weight behind the relentless pressure.

Their hands, slippery with blood, shook with tension. Race braced his left elbow against the canyon wall as he gradually worked his right between their bodies. Letting his knife hand yield a little, then a little more, he quietly guided Jackson's blade. When the Bowie was directly above his own right forearm, Race yielded altogether. A look of ragged pain tore across his face.

Feeling Race's resistance give and seeing that agony cross the cowboy's face, Jackson yelped in triumph. His wild exultation was short-lived as the truth drilled home.

Instead of being buried in Race's chest as Jackson first believed, the Bowie was wedged between the two long bones of Race's forearm.

Clenching his teeth against the searing pain, Race twisted his wrist, solidly jamming the knife in place. Eyes wide with panic, Jackson let go Race's hands to grab the Bowie to free it.

In that glittering instant, Race drove home Jésus' *cuchillo*. Thumb against the knife-guard for extra leverage, Race forced the pointed blade up under Jackson's breastbone and twisted.

A savage satisfaction whipped through Race as he whispered into the killer's ear, "Jackson, you bastard . . . you been *froze out*!"

ZANE GREY'S FAMOUS CHARACTERS LIVE ON IN LEISURE'S ACTION-PACKED WESTERN SERIES BY HIS SON, ROMER ZANE GREY

MORE HARD-RIDING, STRAIGHT-SHOOTING WESTERN ADVENTURE FROM LEISURE BOOKS

Make the Most of Your Leisure Time with
LEISURE BOOKS

Please send me the following titles:

Quantity	Book Number	Price
_____	_____	_____
_____	_____	_____
_____	_____	_____
_____	_____	_____
_____	_____	_____

If out of stock on any of the above titles, please send me the alternate title(s) listed below:

_____	_____	_____
_____	_____	_____
_____	_____	_____

Postage & Handling   _____

Total Enclosed $_____

☐ Please send me a free catalog.

NAME _____
(please print)

ADDRESS _____

CITY _____ STATE _____ ZIP _____

Please include $1.00 shipping and handling for the first book ordered and 25¢ for each book thereafter in the same order. All orders are shipped within approximately 4 weeks via postal service book rate. PAYMENT MUST ACCOMPANY ALL ORDERS.*

*Canadian orders must be paid in US dollars payable through a New York banking facility.

Mail coupon to: **Dorchester Publishing Co., Inc.**
6 East 39 Street, Suite 900
New York, NY 10016
Att: ORDER DEPT.